Straight Into Darkness

MUSIC OF THE AMERICAN SOUTH

Straight Into Darkness

Tom Petty
as Rock Mystic

Megan Volpert

The University of Georgia Press
Athens

© 2022 by the University of Georgia Press
Athens, Georgia 30602
www.ugapress.org
All rights reserved
Designed by Rebecca A. Norton
Set in Adobe Jenson Pro 11/15

Most University of Georgia Press titles are
available from popular e-book vendors.

Printed digitally

Library of Congress Cataloging-in-Publication Data
Names: Volpert, Megan A., author.
Title: Straight into darkness : Tom Petty as rock mystic / Megan Volpert.
Description: Athens : The University of Georgia Press, 2022. | Series: Music of the
American South | Includes bibliographical references.
Identifiers: LCCN 2022005745 | ISBN 9780820362465 (paperback) |
ISBN 9780820362472 (ebook)
Subjects: LCSH: Petty, Tom—Criticism and interpretation. |
Petty, Tom. Straight Into Darkness. | Petty, Tom. Long after dark. |
Rock music—1981–1990—History and criticism.
Classification: LCC ML410.P3135 V65 2022 | ddc 782.42166092—dc23/eng/20220223
LC record available at https://lccn.loc.gov/2022005745

A blind man eager to see who knows that the night has no end,
he is still on the go. The rock is still rolling.

ALBERT CAMUS, *The Myth of Sisyphus*

Contents

Straight Into Darkness

Introduction

No way around it: I once was carrying so much physical chronic pain that I got near to jumping off a train platform, but I didn't because of Tom Petty's "Straight Into Darkness." This little book examines why.

The number of good books about Petty can be counted on one hand. Most of them are properly researched journalistic enterprises that shy away from too many critical maneuvers, like examining the nitty-gritty of his word choices or arguing about whether his work is kind to women. None of them much illuminates the nature of a personal connection between author and subject, and none of them explicitly dips a toe into any philosophy. I hope the form and content of what I'm doing here stands for something new, and I'm sure a lot of folks won't like it.

That's got to be all right, that uncertainty and distaste for innovative approaches to a beloved thing. There are lots of salvation songs in this world—and even many others in the Petty catalog to which countless strangers have doubtless given their allegiance. But as I stood over those train tracks preparing to surrender to disease and despair in the psychedelic blindness of my simple human misery, the one song out of hundreds of available Heartbreakers tracks that came through my headphones at that one perfect moment was "Straight Into Darkness." I've built my life around this epiphany, so it seems like a decent thing to build a book around too. At least you know that I mean what I say, that you can believe me because of the debt I owe to the song.

It has to be paid forward because it can't be paid back—because just as I was finishing up writing these essays in autumn of 2017, Tom Petty died. The first thing I thought to myself was the same thing Jerry Garcia is rumored to have said when Pig Pen died: "That fucker. Now he *knows*." At first, nobody was sure Petty had really died. There was another time the celebrity gossip press declared him deceased and it wasn't true. This round, my newspaper students scooped me on it, for which I paused long enough to be proud of them before kind of mourning. It was confirmed that he was taken off life support but not that he actually died. I fell asleep on Atlanta time that night while Petty played Schrödinger's cat in Los Angeles. Of even the most basic facts, with Petty you could never quite be certain. He really liked that about himself, I'll bet. I wouldn't exactly know because we never met, and now—at least in this lifetime—we won't.

But Petty is possessed of some of that type of fan who has advanced beyond mere biographical litanies to a space of psychoanalysis and ultimately commiseration that borders on a lifetime parasocial partnership. I mean like prophets have. He seldom capitalized on that, even though he could've been an out-and-out preacher alongside Bruce Springsteen if he'd wanted. He just kept his head down, always working, to a point where, despite the uncertainties generated by his ornery personality, the steadfastness of his labor was mythic. A happy Sisyphus.

From an active band's perspective, Petty basically picked a great time to go: one week after the wrap on his fortieth-anniversary tour, a victory lap if ever there was one; his ideas for the rerelease of *Wildflowers* on record, enough for that launch to go as he wished it when the dust settled; his revival of Mudcrutch including a surprise hit single; honored a few months prior as MusiCares' Person of the Year for his decades of charitable work; loved well by his wife Dana for so long; at the mystical, round, rock 'n' roll age of sixty-six.

Before his death was confirmed, it was reported that a hospital chaplain had been called to the room earlier that morning, as Petty was not expected to live through the day. I found the provision of this one detail so extraordinary. Petty was stone-cold guarded on issues as private as his religion, though he was vaguely known to favor meditation. Even the simple acknowledgment of a chaplain's presence feels thick with implication. But don't go getting all sad that the man died as you read through these essays. I sure was hoping Petty would get to read this book, and maybe his ghost can dig it, but his death changes no part of what I have to say about his life's work. As Albert Camus said, "If this myth is tragic, that is because the hero is conscious. Sisyphus, proletarian of the gods, powerless and rebellious, knows the whole extent of his wretched condition: it is what he thinks of during his decent. The lucidity that was to constitute his torture at the same time crowns his victory. There is no fate that cannot be surmounted by scorn."

Somebody else can do the chronological summary. Somebody else can do the rundown of Petty's legacy in the music industry. Whatever you came here looking for, I wish you luck finding it.

You're welcome to skip around in this book. Each essay is a self-contained unit, but the essays are also sorted into six tools for approaching the song—personally, musically, historically, rhetorically, sociologically, and philosophically. The five chapters on the band's fortieth-anniversary tour comprise my thoughts on the challenge of wanting to hear my song at a show. Spoiler alert: I never did. But I did learn to play it myself, which is covered in the section on song composition. You don't need to know a lick of music theory to enjoy this book.

The three chapters on album context provide a condensed version of the Heartbreakers' history as background to understanding the creation of *Long After Dark* and the place of "Straight Into Darkness." The seven chapters on lyrical analysis go through each and every word of the song to get at its many meanings. There are three chapters on mob scene for a sociological and psychological examination of the band's concerts, with a close look at the roles of violence and mysticism. Then the three chapters on standards evaluate philosophical implications of the song as they pertain to individualism, transcendentalism, and absurdism. There's also some good stuff in that section for fans of Bob Dylan, and the occasional whiff of Bruce Springsteen. Overall, I've been neck-deep in the philosophy of Tom Petty for years now and my intention in writing this book is that it provide a way to preach the gospel he taught me.

Firstly, don't believe the good times are over. Petty worked like a madman, enduring the cycle of making albums and then hitting the road to perform them for forty years. Whether it was an odd-numbered year or an even one, you could pretty much set a clock by his launch and tour schedule. He had a firm faith that the next record would be different from and better than the previous one, no matter how many people bought the album or whether it charted or where it got radio play or if it got love from the critics.

He hunted down the good times and gave the finger to whatsoever might get in the way, including the challenge of finishing high school in a timely manner, the necessity of holding a regular job in the early days before Gainesville anointed him, and his wife's unexpected pregnancy just as he was preparing to head out to Los Angeles in search of a recording contract. Even catapulted into serious drug abuse by the end of his first marriage, he rolled into the studio just the same. And he was sought after as a fountain of youth for the good times rock 'n' roll work could afford, a magnet for his elders—Del Shannon, Johnny Cash, Roger McGuinn, George Harrison, Bob Dylan. He worked his ass off as the front of Dylan's backing band. Dylan, who couldn't be bothered to comment for days when the Nobel Committee offered him its prize, responded immediately to the news of Petty's last day, saying, "I thought the world of Tom. He was a great performer, full of the light." The light.

Secondly, don't believe the thrill is all gone. Petty fought like an underdog, speaking up in ways that frequently proved unpopular, even and perhaps especially when he was in the right. He fought for his publishing rights and won freedom from a garbage contract. He hid the master studio tapes even from himself so that no court could force him to fork over an album the record company didn't deserve. He fought to keep the industry from inflating his album pricing and won, chilling price inflation for quite a while across the board. He made fun of Century City and all the lawyers in their glass castles ruining rock 'n' roll through commodification.

He devoted an entire album to bitterly characterizing the failures of contemporary rock radio and its corporate machinations, and continued to be proud of the messaging in *The Last DJ* even though the album tanked. He sought absolute creative control from the moment he got in the van and drove to Los Angeles in search of a contract. Work was his good time, and he wouldn't let anyone steal his thrills. Petty hated to be told what do, and if he once maybe stabbed a boardroom table with a switchblade, that was just his way of making it plain by his actions once it seemed that his words hadn't been heard. He took no shit and could smell it coming a mile away.

Thirdly, real love is our salvation. Petty was a fiercely loyal man. He bailed out of a serious corporate contract offer to go with Shelter, a comparatively small potatoes operation, because he hit it off with Denny Cordell on the phone. He stuck with it long after Cordell began neglecting his eager protégé and spending more time in the office than in the studio. He may be the only rock star to have never gotten fed up with the antics of his pal Stevie Nicks. Petty said very little about the reasons for the end of his first marriage, and never spoke ill of Jane when it was over, even though everyone hints around that those twenty-two years of marriage dragged on for much longer than they should've.

The marriage to his band lasted four decades, with hardly a replacement among them. He kept two drummers for twenty years apiece—same with his bassists. During Howie Epstein's ultimately fatal heroin addiction, Petty was so determined to keep the band together that Epstein's tenure still ran across two decades. When some idiot set his house on fire, Petty rescued the Gibson Dove on which nearly all of his songs had been written. He spent thirty years onstage with a perfectly worn out set of Rickenbacker Rose Morris guitars.

And fourth, the strong will carry on. Petty laughed at that which would otherwise have made him rage. He channeled anger into ambition. His father served as a role model of what not to do in this life, letting the bottomless fear and hostility of his working-class feelings turn him into something weak and ineffectual, a joke. When the corporate machine demanded Petty promote his work with crass commercialism, he instead turned in some of the most innovative videography the music industry had ever seen. Hilariously, he ended up making MTV great in its early days.

No telling what all he and George Harrison might goof around about; they both had an instinct for rooting out ironies. When they formed a band together, Petty knew himself to be the littlest big shot in the Traveling Wilburys, so when they all picked silly names, he tacked Junior on the end of his just to look the fact in the eye. He gave voice to Lucky's redneck punch lines on *King of the Hill* and knocked his own toe off on an episode of *The Simpsons*. And let's not forget about all the black humor in his lyrics, many of which were improvised—"God's Gift to Man," "Yer So Bad," "Gator on the Lawn," "A Mind With A Heart Of Its Own," "Spike," and "Heartbreaker's Beach Party," just for starters.

So that's it. Those are the four things Tom Petty taught me that saved my life, each lesson traced back to a line in the bridge verse of "Straight Into Darkness." Done in any number of other ways, I could've ended up working on this book the whole rest of my life over thousands of pages. Hell, I suppose that's what I'm doing anyway. But that's between me and my rock and roller. There's so much more, of course, but I *lived* it and I can write about it until the second coming of Tom Petty and you still won't understand what the fuck I'm talking about until you pony up for the experience of it all for yourself—to live by his example, because rock 'n' roll is a church and Tom Petty was one of my priests. He was a spiritual gangster and then he died. He went straight into darkness and I am still here, very much alive.

Album Context

Up until 1981

"Straight Into Darkness" appears on the fifth Tom Petty and the Heartbreakers record, *Long After Dark*. There is a general consensus among fans, the record company, and the band itself that this album kind of sucked. The album was not mixed in a way that kept pushing the big-drum sound of *Damn the Torpedoes*. The record company couldn't hear any singles among those ten tracks, though the promotional success of the "You Got Lucky" video would launch that one song anyway. The RIAA certified it as gold, but the singles never cracked any top slots until the video for "You Got Lucky" garnered some belated love. Fans would wonder what the record was trying to say. The Heartbreakers always felt clear in concert, but inside the studio, something or other there was always a big struggle, ever since their debut.

In the beginning, after Mudcrutch crossed the country to sign with Shelter Records, Denny Cordell immediately scrutinized the rhythm section's ability to get into a proper groove. He thought the groove was the basis of all great records, and drummer Randall Marsh couldn't hack it. Tired of pouring in money with little to show so far for an album, Cordell cut the entire band loose and retained Petty as a solo act. But Petty very much felt himself as a bandleader, and when a gaggle of Gainesville, Florida, musicians found themselves in a studio to mess around at the invitation of keyboardist Benmont Tench one day, Petty showed up with a harmonica and left with his band, the Heartbreakers.

Lead guitarist Mike Campbell came direct from Mudcrutch, having been invited to team up after Petty was impressed with his rendition of "Johnny B. Goode" at an impromptu, informal audition back in Gainesville. Bassist Ron Blair and drummer Stan Lynch, both of whom had traveled with other bands in Petty's Floridian orbit, were already in Los Angeles working recording sessions. Keyboardist Tench had been performing with Petty since the days of the Sundowners when Tench was just twelve years old. By the time his old pal called Petty in to that fateful session to add some vocals, all the best pieces of Gainesville had fallen into place, and each of them jumped at the chance to join Petty's new outfit.

With their successful next try at a debut album delivered into the hands of the business people, it was time to tour. They went to England as an opening act because they got no traction on the singles in the United States. When that opening act became a headliner, only then did ABC show up with a check to support the financially strapped tour. Petty tore up the check, insulted by its tardiness and tokenism. A second round of radio publicity in the United States helped their debut finally catch fire, and the pressure was on to record a follow-up of the same caliber.

Again they struggled in the studio. Petty wanted to deviate from the debut album in some way, but there was no time to flesh out a target toward which they could aim changes. Cordell was already stepping back into the business side of Shelter, spending a lot of time on the phone in the other Shelter building next door to the studio. With a lack of direction and a shortage of collaborators, other than acid-addled producer Noah Shark, *You're Gonna Get It!* faced lukewarm critical reception, and its singles did not rank as high on the charts as those from the debut had.

Another general consensus is that the third record, *Damn the Torpedoes*, changed everything. To even get the record made was a tremendous uphill battle. Petty had found proper management in Tony Dimitriades and came to understand all the many ways his Shelter contract was designed to keep the band from making any money. These were legendary legal entanglements—they'd signed away their publishing royalties out of a naive eagerness to start recording, they'd been sold to MCA without their consent, the entire band was strapped for cash, and Petty had been taking an equal share of their meager profits despite doing all the administrative legwork with the business side of their operation while the other guys sat around the swimming pool. They were trapped in a bad situation and Petty's lawyers pulled out the lynchpin by declaring him bankrupt.

The entire music industry watched and waited for the outcome of these interwoven complaints, which would set an important precedent. Eventually, Petty was victorious. Biographer Warren Zanes remarked, "The lawsuit revealed something about just who Tom Petty was, his identity as an artist and a man. . . . There was no mythology attached to Tom Petty, and he never tried to build one. But this episode gave the audience, the press, even Petty himself, something to consider. Petty had to make a sacrifice in order to take all of these steps forward, and that was his relationship with Denny Cordell. Petty had lost a mentor, but gained a sense of self."

These legal battles took place throughout the production of *Damn the Torpedoes*, which was financed independently so that the record company couldn't grab it out from under them. Bugs Weidel, their faithful roadie, would load up his trunk with the master tapes and stash them who-knows-where every night, only to bring them back the next morning, to ensure that the record execs had no way to confiscate the album. Though the courtroom battle was harrowing, the band's time in the studio was also extremely fraught, the sound inching along by tooth and nail. The result was a major breakthrough—their first top ten album held steady in the number two slot for seven weeks, topped only by Pink Floyd's *The Wall*. For once, the band got universal critical admiration. Petty said, "On that album, we came up with that big drum sound. That I think, after that, was really imitated everywhere. I think that record changed drum sounds for a long time." This brings us to producer Jimmy Iovine.

Iovine was a college dropout from Brooklyn who parlayed a janitorial job into a staff position at Brooklyn's Record Plant studio. By 1978, he was best known as an engineer on Bruce Springsteen's *Born to Run* and the producer for Patti Smith's *Easter*. Petty had intended him to be an engineer, but Iovine brought along his own engineer and quickly established a common wavelength with Petty for how the two of them could steer the record together. Iovine's enthusiasm was infectious, and the band was swept up in his methods, which were even more exacting than what they'd learned from Cordell and Shark. Petty and Iovine shared a grand vision; both of them felt the pressure to make something truly excellent, lest their careers face an early plateau. As Zanes noted, "If the first two records took significant effort, the third was taxing on another level. It was less about joy than ambition." And that pioneering drum sound had to be wrestled out of Stan Lynch.

Petty said, "In the studio it could be quite difficult with Stan because he wasn't really a studio drummer, and he didn't like the idea of sometimes being cut back to just playing time." According to Weidel, "Live, Stan was a great drummer. He's brilliant. But especially in the studio, these guys were almost clinical. . . . That was the tradition from early on, maybe not the second record but by *Damn the Torpedoes*: start recording to record, kind of hit a brick wall, fire Stanley, go a little further, hire Stanley back, make the record. That went on several times." Petty said Iovine was "*really* tough on Stan. *Really* tough. They did not get along" and that Iovine "just couldn't understand why Stan wasn't fired."

Iovine was a drill sergeant, and, Petty said, "I remember taking a *day* to get a snare drum sound. That, to us, was just *outrageous*. Took a whole day to get a drum sound. It was really boring and hard to understand. But we got there." It was hard on all the Heartbreakers to be stuck in the room for that. Campbell said of this period in the studio that "it's the only time I've walked out of a session." As early as the *Damn the Torpedoes* recording sessions, Zanes said Campbell wasn't alone in this, that bassist Ron Blair "was already drifting away, discouraged by the way his friends changed when their dreams started coming true."

Their follow-up to this triple-platinum third album was *Hard Promises*, which Petty said "is when this became a job as well. It became a job, it had to be done. [*Laughs*] Which is the first time that it really hit me that way. That this *has* to be done, and it *has* to be good, and it *has* to be successful. Which really ain't the way to go about it. So it wasn't as much fun, that record, as the one before it." The Heartbreakers wanted the studio to stay fun, but the album had to sound different once again. Petty said, "We always frowned on people that made the same record again with different words or whatever. We were going to try and take it somewhere we hadn't been."

"*Hard Promises* was an extreme example of trying to do something different from *Damn the Torpedoes*, which I think frustrated Jimmy quite a bit. I wanted to start moving away from this anthemic sort of music. There's extreme things on there like 'Something Big' and 'Change Your Mind', and acoustic numbers. It was a little scattered. We worked very hard on it and were under the terrible pressure of following a huge hit," said Petty. But Iovine thought if it ain't broke, you don't fix it. According to the *Playback* liner notes written by Bill Flanagan, "*Hard Promises* had represented something of a tug-of-war between Petty and producer Iovine. Restless as always, Petty had wanted to pull away from the studio craft of *Torpedoes*, while Iovine thought it was nuts to screw with a winning formula. The result was an album that sounded of two minds about itself—was *Hard Promises* a mainstream rock LP with a few eccentricities or the work of a quirky singer/songwriter with a mainstream polish?" Though Iovine eventually rallied as much enthusiasm as he had for *Torpedoes*, even to the point of believing *Hard Promises* could top it, he still made a clear division between the marketable singles, which he would care about intensely, versus Petty's interest in telling stories, which he utterly dismissed as "the Dylan thing."

When the album was finished, Petty would face the recording industry behemoth once again, this time in the name of pricing. MCA was testing the waters, seeing how much fans would pay for their rock star's next album. Steely Dan's *Goucho* and the *Xanadu* soundtrack featuring Electric Light Orchestra with Olivia Newton-John had been rolled out at $9.89—upcharging by one dollar from previous album pricing. *Hard Promises* would have been the next trial balloon if Petty hadn't raised such an enormously public stink about it. In the end, he got his way and dodged the price hike, and said, "I was proud that I pulled it off, but what I was not happy with was that I had just been through all that legal trouble with *Damn the Torpedoes*, and I found myself right back in a record-company conflict. I think it wore on me pretty bad at that time."

After the studio struggle and the business struggle, next came the touring struggle. Petty lost his voice onstage, which was diagnosed first as laryngitis, then, after a few days of unsuccessful rest, as tonsillitis. Petty said of the incident, "That really affected me mentally for *years*. It just *terrified* me, the idea of going onstage and not being able to sing. I still deal with it, to some degree. It traumatized me. And so, yeah, I was actually put in the hospital and had my tonsils removed in the midst of a tour. And that, with the price thing, is when I *really* realized that being famous can be hard." Uncertainty had proliferated across all facets of the one thing to which Petty had devoted his whole life.

Hard Promises was destined to live in the quadruple-platinum shadow of Stevie Nicks's solo debut, *Bella Donna*. Nicks rose to prominence on two wildly successful Fleetwood Mac albums, but after they released the comparative failure of *Tusk* in 1979, the frustration of accommodating three songwriters on each album left her with a surplus of good material to launch on her own. Iovine was still working with the Heartbreakers, but he'd begun dating Nicks and also working on her album. The couple prevailed upon Petty to give Nicks a single for her record. His "Stop Draggin' My Heart Around" duet on *Bella Donna* would top the charts, and, ironically, block the singles on his own album from getting much play. Radio producers couldn't see the sense in promoting "A Woman In Love (But It's Not Me)" or "The Waiting" when Petty's voice was already airing every hour on the track that belonged to Nicks. Beyond gifting her a number one song, there is at least one Heartbreaker playing on nine out of the album's ten tracks.

Here was a band that seemed to always get in its own way somehow. The mission was so simple, but the logistics were convoluted: there were clashing visions and difficult personalities in the studio; the tour kind of choked; Stevie Nicks was getting the boost from Petty's killer single at his own expense; and things were looking pretty bleak in 1981, when it came time to turn their attention toward *Long After Dark*.

Making the Album

Long After Dark marked several crossroads moments for the Heart-breakers. It was their last album for Backstreet under the terms of the *Damn the Torpedoes* legal settlement. It was the band's last album produced in full by Jimmy Iovine, though Petty would later call him back to work on bits and pieces. Most importantly, it was the first record on which bassist Howie Epstein replaced Ron Blair. Petty "stole" Epstein from Del Shannon while producing his *Drop Down and Get Me* comeback album. The Heartbreakers had been called in as Shannon's backing band, so the audition happened organically once it was announced that Blair was calling it quits.

Said Blair, "I've told this story probably twelve different ways, and it could go anywhere from *If I was fired, I probably deserved it* to *My mind left planet Band* to *I needed a break*. But there was a pivotal moment for me." He got a phone call from Dimitriades and they agreed things had soured. Zanes said the whole band saw it coming: "No one in or around the band denies that as of 1981, Ron Blair was drifting. He wasn't behaving like a band member. He'd taken a stroll to the periphery, and it left him vulnerable." Show biz was getting to him: "The way we'd talk about other people and other bands. You know, 'Our gang is better than your gang.' The competition and the gossip. It just rubbed me the wrong way, the way the game is played."

Petty sympathized: "[Ron] was very sincere. He quit the music business *completely*. Something had popped, and he didn't want to play music at all." Yet, as Zanes noted, "A vacancy in the band was a problem with historical reverberations." If the band could carry on at all, a new bassist would certainly mean a different sound. But Blair's absence was perhaps most impactful on the remainder of the rhythm section. Said Zanes, "With Blair gone, there was no band member Lynch could use to distract the others, and shield himself, from the painful attention he got in the studio as the drummer who wasn't always giving the band what they wanted."

Beyond drumming, Lynch was the primary band member responsible for singing harmonies, and Epstein would take that away from him. According to Bill Flanagan, "Epstein had two qualities Petty valued highly: he had no ego problems and he could sing his butt off." Campbell confirmed both attributes: "Howie came in and was a great harmony singer, which was the main thing he brought to us. Howie played the bass more like a guitar player or a singer who was accompanying his voice."

Epstein was accustomed to playing studio sessions and was glad to contribute whatever the band could use. He said, "If somebody else comes up with a better part, great. I don't get bothered by that at all. I know some people do. 'I'm the bass player!' I think that's kind of silly. If Ben or whoever comes up with a better bass part, we'd be fools not to use it. I was definitely happy when I joined the band. I really think it was stranger for them. I don't think the guys had been in many other bands. They were so close knit, where I was used to playing with lots of bands. I think it was a little weird for them to have this new guy in there."

By contrast, Lynch was more unsatisfied than ever. In addition to the familiar trouble posed by Iovine's intense methods, the drummer was also less than pleased with Petty's newfound interest in punching up the songs by slightly speeding up many of the mixes: "They went through the rectum of the fourth dimension and never came back. I say if you want to make a rock-and-roll record, you've got to let some feathers fly. The control issues at that point were way beyond reason." Lynch increasingly dropped off from the studio work and would quit the band entirely in 1994.

Petty and Iovine likewise couldn't agree on a sound for the record. According to Flanagan, "Nobody was entirely satisfied with the result [of *Hard Promises*], and Iovine argued hard for going back to the formula that had served them so well on *Torpedoes*. The next album, 1983's *Long After Dark*, was at least superficially an attempt to do that. But in his heart Petty could not understand why he would ever want to repeat himself and on that album he struggled against Iovine's structures. One result is that the songwriting on *Long After Dark*, if not the sound and arrangements, is among Petty's bleakest."

Of the nineteen songs recorded during the *Long After Dark* studio sessions, only ten appeared on the album. Petty said, "There were songs being left off that record that were really good [because] Jimmy and I were butting heads at that point. . . . I didn't think Jimmy was experimental enough. I think he was playing it too safe." Iovine always had an ear for the radio singles, while Petty was diving deeper into his Dylanesque mode of storytelling. Petty said, "Iovine felt I had gone too far afield on *Hard Promises* and wanted to get back to a good rockin' record. I became bored with that really quick. It was a tough record for me. If you listen to the outtakes from that album—'Keeping Me Alive,' 'Turning Point'—that was really where I was heading at the time. And those songs were completely dismissed, they weren't even considered for that album."

Iovine discouraged what he perceived as country tendencies in the new material. Said Petty, "I didn't see them as country songs. I saw them as something a little more organic, more acoustic-oriented than we had done. I think I would have really liked to go in that direction. He didn't like the idea of it. So I think I finally gave in to the way he was thinking. But I think it would have helped that record to have those songs on it." The band subsequently put four of the album's ten tracks on the second disc of the *Playback* collection, appropriately titled "Spoiled and Mistreated." *Long After Dark* marks the point when Petty saw Iovine turning away from the creative side, precisely as Cordell had done: "I really think Iovine wanted to be a businessman by that point. Maybe I'm wrong, but by '82, I think Jimmy was on the phone more than he was in the studio."

According to Flanagan, Petty "felt that he had allowed himself to be painted into a musical corner, and even when he and the Heartbreakers succeeded in busting out with a 'You Can Still Change Your Mind' or 'Something Big,' they were told that such tracks could not be singles because it was not what the public expected from Tom Petty and the Heartbreakers." Petty has a history of protesting that hitmaker mentality: "I don't know if our best work has always been the single." In the end, he had profound regrets about the way *Long After Dark* turned out. He said, "I felt that we were making the wrong decisions all the time. . . . I went along with it and I think I was wrong. I should have stood up for myself. Jimmy had nothing but our best interests in mind and we respected him enough to go along with his ideas. It's a fine album but to me it was treading water, we'd been down that road before."

On the other hand, it was hard to fight against Iovine's direction when Petty had no clear vision of his own. He said, "It was a tough record, because I never knew what it was." One element he always did emphasize was song sequencing: "I don't know how many people take the time to sit down and listen to an album straight through anymore—but I do. And I look at it that way when I'm making one, too. It's a piece unto itself. It has a beginning, a middle and an end. That's the art of making an album."

The sequence on *Long After Dark* runs itself in circles. "One Story Town" opens the album by applauding a girl who broke free of her small-town fate, but the chorus reminds us the speaker is still trapped there. "You Got Lucky" celebrates good loving but questions whether there's ever better loving out there somewhere else. The speaker of "Deliver Me" asks to be taken in by the same love he just told to go. In "Change of Heart," he's the one doing the leaving this time. In "Finding Out," he's back again, allegedly with a better handle on what love really means. So that's Side A: will they or won't they get together, and can they or should they stay together?

Side B is the same story told by a similarly jumbled collage. "We Stand a Chance," but will she let him prove it? Things are very uncertain when we go "Straight Into Darkness." He thought they could really make it, but turns out it was "The Same Old You." Now he's caught "Between Two Worlds" because he's hung up on something that is bad for him. He's still sort of rooting for the girl and he might even come around again, but he mainly just hopes she doesn't have "A Wasted Life."

Playback supplies two of the nine tracks that went missing from the final cut of *Long After Dark*: "Keeping Me Alive" and "Turning Point." Petty wrote "Keeping Me Alive" in the style of his heroes, the Everly Brothers: "The Everly Brothers songs aren't real deep on the surface, but they say so much about the times—and sometimes the innocence is a bit naughty." With its working-class lament in contrast to the untroubled gratitude for a girl by his side, "Keeping Me Alive" manages to go several notches sunnier than "Deliver Me" while maintaining a similarly looming background scene. The tempo of "Turning Point" seems fairly upbeat, yet the lyrics convey ambiguous and unending struggle: "It's almost Buddy Holly–ish, or an 'I Fought the Law' kind of feel. It's kind of an ominous song, though I think an optimistic one. I thought it hung together really well and had really great changes, great tension."

It's impossible to guess where these two tracks might have fallen in the lineup if they'd made the final cut. The song sequence is cyclical, and the stories don't seem to have any climaxes. Everything here is stuck in the middle, searching for a proper beginning or ending. Even Petty's characterization of the outtakes speaks to this—there are tremendous ironies in "Turning Point" being left off the album. A song is innocent but still naughty, or ominous but optimistic. The great tension he sought for the songs of *Long After Dark* was holding up a mirror, a confused and inadvertent reveal of the ambivalence he felt toward the practical reality of his calling as a musician. By this time, he understood the trap of the album cycle, and *Long After Dark* is a showcase for his frightened fatigue.

Promoting the Album

Long After Dark is too often waved away as perhaps the least notable album Petty ever made. Even albums like *The Last DJ* or *Echo* are given more attention because at least the former is a controversial knock at the music business and the latter is a testament to Petty's personal struggles with divorce and heroin. *Long After Dark* is worthy of more intense consideration because it marks an end—after which would come different producers, collaborations with many of Petty's elders, solo albums, and other serious stabs at newness or reinvention.

This fifth album bookmarks 1982 as Petty's reckoning with the absurd, with the ceaselessly repetitive and uselessly empty cycle of success for a rock star. He began to worry about the trap of "his years living inside the album cycle." According to Zanes, Petty would "write the songs, go into the studio, make the record, mix it and master it, set up the release, do press, tour behind the record, write the songs, go into the studio, make the record . . . and thirty years later, if you're lucky enough to *get* that many years, your kids are grown-ups. Petty has spent most of his life at work." Journalist Steve Pond reported that it was driving Petty mad, into a time of prolific waste: "For months, the schedule was monotonous: record, break while Petty wrote more songs, record, break. The band would tell Petty to write one song, and he'd return with five. The record had too many rockers; Petty would go home and write ballads. When there got to be too many ballads, he started ditching them like crazy. 'I was trying to find the right balance,' he says."

He was overdoing it with no results, looking for balance but finding monotony. The album was yielding nothing new. We've got to get heavy to discuss the philosophical implications of this, to give proper weight to *Long After Dark* as the primary example of how Petty navigated an existential crisis. As Albert Camus acknowledged in *The Myth of Sisyphus*, "It happens that the stage sets collapse." His description of daily monotony rivals Zanes's descriptions of the album cycle:

> Rising, street-car, four hours in the office or factory, meal, street-car, four hours of work, meal, sleep, and Monday Tuesday Wednesday Thursday Friday and Saturday according to the same rhythm—this path is easily followed most of the time. But one day the "why" arises and everything begins in that weariness tinged with amazement. "Begins"—this is important. Weariness comes at the end of the acts of a mechanical life, but at the same time it inaugurates the impulse of consciousness. It awakens consciousness and provokes what follows. What follows is the gradual return into the chain or it is the definitive awakening. At the end of the awakening comes, in time, the consequence: suicide or recovery.

Petty's weariness with *Long After Dark* therefore functions as proof that he had finally and totally awakened to the absurdity of stardom. As Camus defined it, "This divorce between man and his life, the actor and his setting, is properly the feeling of absurdity. All healthy men having thought of their own suicide, it can be seen, without further explanation, that there is a direct connection between this feeling and the longing for death." Whether Petty would recover from his crisis of stardom consciousness or suicidally drive his music career into the ground remained to be seen in 1982, but he was on the precipice of the only line of inquiry that ever mattered to existentialism, since "judging whether life is or is not worth living amounts to answering the fundamental question of philosophy."

The instinctual nature of this moment is pretty dangerous because "an act like this is prepared within the silence of the heart, as is a great work of art. The man himself is ignorant of it." Petty's passion for making great music, according to Camus, is located in the same spot as our human impulse to end it all with self-sabotage. He was trying to pour all this rock and roll mojo into *Long After Dark*, but it wouldn't gel. It had no resonance for him, despite his labor: "At this point in his effort man stands face to face with the irrational," said Camus. "He feels within him his longing for happiness and for reason. The absurd is born of this confrontation between the human need and the unreasonable silence of the world."

A musician can walk away from this darkness, from the world that won't properly answer back. But then the music itself is lost, so the issue is whether Petty was called to music to such an extent that he would refuse to walk away from it, even though producing this music was precisely the thing causing him so much pain: "From the moment absurdity is recognized, it becomes a passion, the most harrowing of all. But whether or not one can live with one's passions, whether or not one can accept their law, which is to burn the heart they simultaneously exalt—that is the whole question."

He didn't walk away; he picked up the problem and ran with it. Zanes said that the "almost ceaseless movement between writing, recording, going home to his family, and working through the band's affairs had begun to define who he was. He was a workingman. The old gang wasn't the same because, as he put it, 'Someone had to be the adult here.'" To lead a band is to assume responsibility for its challenges, perhaps especially its existential ones. Zanes said specifically of *Long After Dark* that making the album was "a matter of Petty wanting to avoid trouble that might come from the guys he'd known since high school, while recognizing that he'd been in that situation for years. He couldn't have what he thought of as a real band and *not* find himself there. But the fatigue of that and the fatigue of the album cycle itself were both weighing on Petty. The Heartbreakers, too, were struggling with the relentlessness and its cumulative effects."

What Petty knew instinctively of the Heartbreakers' ups and downs thus far was that "if the descent is thus sometimes performed in sorrow, it can also take place in joy." To shift toward darkness as a metaphor for the same, Camus said, "There is no sun without shadow, and it is essential to know the night. The absurd man says yes and his efforts will henceforth be unceasing." Petty went straight into that darkness and met the relentlessness of absurdity with his unceasing work. He finished *Long After Dark* by taking joy in writing through his existential crisis. Camus said, "One does not discover the absurd without being tempted to write a manual of happiness." The clearest example of such a manual on *Long After Dark* is "Straight Into Darkness."

Journalist Bill Flanagan remarked of the album, "I really thought it might be his best. 'Straight Into Darkness' hit me very powerfully. But looking back, knowing what we know about all that would come, it feels too much like they're at risk of repeating the formula. They're going to loosen up. But it happens after that album." Petty similarly appraised "Straight Into Darkness" as a "really, really good song. I think that was a better record than we got credit for at the time. It's like, oh yeah, they've got a hit song on the radio, but it wasn't really applauded. What am I to do? Spoiled and mistreated, right?" Of the totality of the album, he concluded, "I think it's a good album. The last time I heard it, it was pretty good. The only thing I could say that I didn't like about it was that it wasn't really going forward enough for me. I think it's imperative that you move everything forward with each recording. It was sort of a 'tread water' album. We're doing what we're supposed to do here—not really going forward."

Yet they plunged headlong into the tour: "The Heartbreakers got on a leased plane, the Phantom, with a line from *Long After Dark's* 'The

Same Old You' painted on the side: 'Let That Sucker Blast.' Off they went, into America to play those songs." The tagline on the side of the Phantom was about the joys of life on the road. Indeed, the Heartbreakers always got more excited for their cycle to swing toward touring, away from recording. The tour was weirdly sponsored by Tecate beer, but the band needed stronger stuff to push their existential crisis into any kind of remission. Tench said, "On the *Long After Dark* tour, I discovered how much cocaine there was in the world." By the time the tour was wrapping up, Petty said, "I started to take it all too seriously. I really wanted to part the Red Sea every night. I felt I had to. If we hadn't taken the break, I think we might have split up because I was bored." Mike Campbell called the break after this tour "the dark period." Campbell checked himself into the hospital for exhaustion, and Tench went to rehab for drugs and alcohol. Said Camus, "In a man's attachment to life there is something stronger than all the ills of this world. The body's attachment is as good as the mind's, and the body shrinks from annihilation."

They hadn't quite run themselves into the ground completely, but they had each pushed it pretty close. Said Camus, "Killing yourself amounts to confessing. It is confessing that life is too much for you or that you do not understand it. It is merely confessing that that 'is not worth the trouble.' Living, naturally, is never easy." Touring isn't easy either, perhaps especially when supporting a lackluster album. Yet, "in order to keep alive, the absurd cannot be settled. It escapes suicide to the extent that it is simultaneously awareness and rejection of death." So the Heartbreakers went on a break, their unsettled fate underscored by a less-than-blockbuster tour.

During this break the band ironically managed to catapult itself into massively public view through MTV. Petty said "You Got Lucky" was "the most misunderstood song I ever wrote" because listeners mistake the speaker's sarcasm for chauvinism. It reached number one on the Billboard Mainstream Rock chart with thanks mainly due to its music video. Petty's old Mudcrutch pal Tom Leadon confirmed Petty's filmic sensibilities from an early age when Petty would fill him in on movies he'd seen: "He'd sit there and spend an hour, tell me the whole movie. The dialogue, the scenes in detail. He did it several times. I was amazed that he could remember all of it. I think it was real to him in a way. Like he was experiencing it." This echoes that same wellspring of storytelling that Jimmy Iovine would later dismiss as "the Dylan thing."

The band had made a handful of other videos before, mainly to get out of doing live appearances on talk shows. Petty said, "Then in 1981, for *Hard Promises*, we did four videos in two days directed by my high-school buddy Jim Lenahan, who did our lighting and staging on tour. 'A Woman in Love' was really good. The Police completely stole that. They stole the cinematographer, Daniel Pearl, the location, everything, for 'Every Breath You Take.' In those days we were actually cutting film by hand in the editing booth, and I was there right through the cut, through everything. So when MTV came along, I was an old hand at it. But I never dreamed those things would be seen repeatedly."

Pearl went on to win MTV's first video cinematography award for "Every Breath You Take," and the song itself went on to the title of biggest single of the year in both the United States and United Kingdom. Said Petty, "'You Got Lucky' was a real groundbreaker. There was a minute-long scene where we walked through the desert, uncover a dusty old boom box, and push play, and that's when the music begins. Michael Jackson called us, saying what an incredible idea that was." Petty emphasized that "it really changed everything. No one had ever—even Michael Jackson—done a prelude to the video." He recalled that "that video was terrific fun. We wrote the treatment ourselves and borrowed a ton from *Mad Max*, something we shared with many videos of that era. That was when we really saw MTV change our daily lives. Not only were teenagers spotting me on the street, older people would spot me, too. We knew it was big."

But the videos suffered from the same overmedicating as the tour did. Said Petty, "There was a lot of coke on the sets of music videos. I found that coke made all the waiting around even more painful. I didn't do it much. But the crews, they were cocaine-powered. Nowadays, I can't bear to look at one of my music videos. I can't stand 'em. I feel like I can taste the cocaine, smell the arc lamps." Tom Petty martyred himself to MTV as what Camus called the absurd hero: "He is, as much through his passions as through his torture. His scorn of the gods, his hatred of death, and his passion for life won him that unspeakable penalty in which the whole being is exerted toward accomplishing nothing. This is the price that must be paid for the passions of this earth." Petty said, "I didn't much like making videos—the hours were insane—but I liked the outcome. My band hated making videos. They didn't want to go anywhere near them. I didn't blame them. But I didn't have a choice. I had to be in them." Having to do the videos was one price that Petty paid for the songs he loved.

And the videos were literally expensive. MTV cofounder John Sykes said, "We got 90 percent of our content for free." Production executive Abbey Konowitch said, "Sykes knew how to build relationships with artists. He was slick, and he got the Rolling Stones and Billy Idol and Tom Petty to do things for free, for a network that barely existed. He was great at getting artists to believe in the dream, and he executed his promotions so brilliantly that artists would say thank you to him when they were over." It was to Petty's credit that he was assigned to Sykes. Another executive, Bob Pittman, recalled that "Les [Garland] and Sykes managed relationships with the music industry. The wild and crazy ones dealt with Les, and the businesslike and analytical ones dealt with Sykes."

Petty said, "I never thought it was fair. MTV was getting programming for free. I was going into the hole *millions* because I had to deliver videos to promote my singles, and they weren't giving anything back.

They looked at it like airplay was your payment, but you weren't guaranteed that airplay." "You Got Lucky" got lucky with an extremely heavy rotation on MTV, and the band's disdain for their own video contributions blossomed quickly into a distaste for what MTV had done to their audience. Petty said, "MTV—I could tell right away that was going to rule out anybody not clever enough to make a video and look good doing it. I adapted. But the audience started to change—I saw people being fed shit and only too happy to eat it."

Said Camus, "The theme of the irrational, as it is conceived by the existentials, is reason becoming confused and escaping by negating itself. The absurd is lucid reasoning noting its limits." "You Got Lucky" ultimately garnered maximum attention due to its prelude—Petty changed the entire landscape of the industry not with his song but with the seventy-two seconds of silence that preceded it. The video itself played on the keyword "luck," with broad Western and sci-fi arcade motifs. Despite the misperceived misogyny of the song's lyrics, the band turned in a video that went against the hypersexualized grain of MTV. Said Petty, "We didn't go for the sexy video girl thing. I knew it would cheapen our long-term play. I wasn't happy the way videos started to exploit women. I thought, we are all better than this, and that the music should do the job."

The cycle of Tom Petty's existence that pertains to *Long After Dark*—writing it, recording it, touring it, promoting it, and otherwise in every possible moment living it—was indeed among his darkest. Camus provides cold comfort in that "at last man will again find there the wine of the absurd and the bread of indifference on which he feeds his greatness. Let us insist again on the method: it is a matter of persisting." *Long After Dark* is a true testament to Petty's greatness, most simply because he persisted in creating it despite its absurdity—despite its repetitiveness of composition, its aimlessness of lyric, the expansive yawn of the audience on tour, and the expensive promotional void of MTV.

We need not speculate about what was on Petty's individual mind in 1982. Said Camus, "It is probably true that a man remains forever unknown to us and that there is in him something irreducible that escapes us, but *practically* I know men and recognize them by their behavior, by the totality of their deeds, by the consequences caused in life by their presence." By this method, we have reason to restore a sense of majesty to *Long After Dark* as we evaluate "Straight Into Darkness" by its consequence for the totality of Petty's later deeds.

Song Composition

Chord Progression

I finally took up guitar in my mid-thirties and still don't know that much about it. Self-teaching is slow going, though most guitarists will tell you it's the only way. Because I'm left-handed, there were a number of tough decisions to make before making any noise: I could play a lefty guitar strung properly, a righty strung upside down, or a righty strung properly. After researching all the greats—Albert King, Jimi Hendrix, Paul Mc-Cartney, Kurt Cobain, and many more—I opted for a lefty guitar strung properly for the simple fact that I always instinctively use my left hand to strum when busting out some air guitar.

The next decision placed even further constraint on me because I'm vain about my hands. With consideration for my long, witchy fingers, my mom always says her biggest regret of my youth was not forcing me to play piano. These hands somehow survived a decade of motorcycling and I wasn't about to put calluses on them to pick at a guitar on weekends. I decided to keep to using a slide and let the metal wrangle the strings.

Despite having played drums in junior high and possessing an ability to keep quick time, I never learned how to read music. Looking at guitar tablature online was like doing math, and I felt as dumb as I did in algebra class back in high school. So I was going to learn where to put the slide to make a chord with my right hand and hope my left would naturally find its way from drumming to strumming.

The first song I learned to play was Chuck Berry's "Johnny B. Goode," and its chords go A-D-E. There's a cool thing about playing slide guitar, which is that your slide hand begins to make little geometric shapes as you move through the chords. Berry's song was just a straight line.

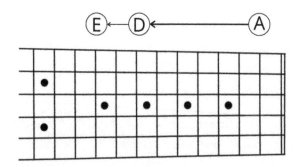

If you play chords using your fingers, you curl your fingers up in all kinds of funny ways that don't seem to me to mean very much. But with a slide, the shapes take on meaning pretty easy and I began to recognize patterns. An A-D-E song could also be played as a G-C-D song. It was the same straight line, beginning on one fret, then moving down to the fourth and then the fifth. This 1-4-5 pattern is one of the most common in songwriting. Some musicians change it up to 4-1-5 or 5-1-4 or 5-4-1, but you get the idea. That pattern of three chords hangs together nicely wherever you want to hit it on the fretboard.

Somebody along the way told me that learning slide in open G tuning was easiest, so that's how I found all the major chords, A to G, just right down the neck, placing the slide on the first fret for A, the second for B, and so on down to the sixth for F. The G was hanging in the air, an open strumming with no need for the slide to do anything on the neck. I really liked thinking about the change of shape made by my slide hand because I saw that not only could I go up and down the frets, but also out from them into that extra dimension of the open G, hovering above them before dropping back down to find other notes. Or I'd get cool triangles by switching up the order of the three chords, like C-G-D instead of G-C-D.

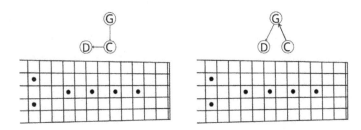

This gifted me plenty of songs, but eventually I ran into minor chords. In a slide situation, a minor chord pretty much just means you strum the heavy bass strings more than the light treble strings. Minor chords are supposed to sound more lowdown and sad. Once you've got minor notes, you can graduate to songs with four chords. Perhaps the most common pattern tacks a minor chord onto the 1-4-5, for a 1-6-4-5 situation where the 6 is minor. So A-D-E becomes A-Fm-D-E and G-C-D becomes G-Em-C-D. Again, you can switch around the order of the notes and it will still sound plenty right.

With mainly these bedrock three- and four-chord progressions, Tom Petty created "Straight Into Darkness." The chorus goes G-D-C, floating on air for G, then dropping down onto the D, and backsliding a little lower into C. The bridge tries to soar with the G over and over again, C-G-D-G-D-G-C, striving for that brass ring, but ultimately ends the way it began. You can play these notes in a bunch of different places on the fretboard if you know how to translate the notes up and down the neck using the patterns they make. It's not very fair to look at how often Petty uses any variation of this three-chord progression because it is just that common. We may as well look at how many times he uses "and" or "the" in his lyrics.

The verses go Em-C-G-D. Petty uses some version of this four-chord progression on one other *Long After Dark* track, "Deliver Me." He also uses it twice on *Hard Promises,* for "A Thing About You" and "Insider." These songs differ widely in tempo, tone, subject matter, and in the many other elements that go into making a song, so it's not necessarily easy to pick up on which ones have similar chord progressions. When I play them back-to-back myself, it's easy to confuse the songs, as my slide hand keeps making variations on the same shape with different pacing.

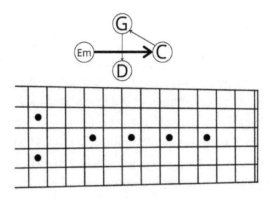

"Straight Into Darkness" begins on that melancholy E-minor note, sinks a little lower to C, only to reach for the stars on an open G, and then comes back down to a compromise point on D midway between the first two notes. That's life in a nutshell: some sadness leans into a deeper pain, we somehow rise above it, and then sink back down into equilibrium until the next hurt, the return of another minor note. The chord progression performs the same message as the lyrics, and makes a nice little mountain to roll your rock up and then watch it slide back down, over and over again.

Arrangement

One common explanation for the failure of *Long After Dark* is that it provides thirty-eight minutes of music with zero minutes of memorable guitar solos. Everyone forgets that memorable opening bars are more this band's thing. Seeing other Florida and Georgia bands meander their way to twelve-minute compositions made Petty impatient from the beginning. Of his southern rock peers, Petty recalled, "Wherever you turned there were dozens of slide guitars jammin' for what seemed like days on end. Things really got quite outta hand and degenerated into tuneless triple live boogie albums." Petty stuck to what he knew from Elvis and the Beatles, doing three or four-minute songs that concentrated on a hook instead of a solo. Mike Campbell had the same philosophy: "The stuff that got me into the guitar . . . the Stones, the Kinks, the Beach Boys, the Animals, all those '60s bands, had real simple guitar parts to go around the song as opposed to guitar solos that interrupted the song."

In a review for *Mojo*, Ben Edmonds remarked, "Campbell's style lies somewhere between self-effacement and in-your-facement, a Clapton who chooses to play more like a McGuinn." The Byrds comparison always delighted Petty, and Campbell knew that Petty often made composition choices with that parallel in mind. Said Campbell, "His way of playing the guitar against a vocal is just right. He sticks in little rhythm things, and when he's singing, he backs off and comps his guitar to the vocal. It balances itself real good. He's real good at that." The producer disapproved of this instinct because of the singer's slurry tendencies, said Petty: "Jimmy Iovine told me, 'People'll never know how good your songs are because you sing like you've got a mouth full of food.' I don't like lyric sheets. Not being able to hear the words clearly gives people the incentive to listen more closely."

Nor could he easily default to following the advice of the producer that had come before Iovine. In teaching Petty how to make a record, Denny Cordell advised Petty that "bass and drums is the foundation of every record you like. You get that right, make a groove, and it's gonna work." Neither drummer nor bassist could really take the lead on this album. Between drummer Stan Lynch's ongoing feud with Iovine and the fact that new bassist Howie Epstein was still learning the ropes, the Heartbreakers leaned on Benmont Tench's piano to get the job done.

Petty's desire to let the lyrics breathe, full of his confusion and frustration as they were, harkened back to the uncertain vibes he had while working through the studio sessions for *Damn the Torpedoes*. One of the lessons of recording at that time was that Tench definitely provided arrangements on which the Heartbreakers could rely. In recording "Refugee," Petty said, "We got there only through the principle of subtraction, meaning what we *didn't* play ultimately meant as much as what we did. Initially we were all trying to do those verses together, with guitars running through the whole thing. But the secret was to let the organ do it alone. Just have the guitars drop out and allow the voice and organ to carry it. That allowed a focus on the intensity of the lyric. That lyric carries a lot of the song's weight and needed space."

Petty's reliance on Tench came and went, and he often sought piano for structure when he was uncertain of how to proceed with a composition, even in the early days of Mudcrutch. The Mudcrutch demo tape contained both a Tench original, "On the Street," and a Petty/Tench cowrite, "Once Upon a Time Somewhere." Warren Zanes said, "You can hear that Benmont Tench is already a highly evolved player, and the band doesn't shy away from putting him right up front." Petty said, "Ben's 'On the Street' was the best thing" on the demo. After Cordell disbanded Mudcrutch in favor of Petty's solo effort, Petty caught Leon Russell's attention in large part due to how he played off of Tench, which Russell was naturally tuned to as a pianist himself. Russell heard Petty's "Lost in Your Eyes" and wanted him to cowrite songs with that same sense of emotionality and believability. Zanes said the song "certainly conveys just how artfully Benmont Tench could come along behind Petty and punctuate every moment of feeling, never overreaching."

After the formation of the Heartbreakers, Tench no longer received any songwriting credits, and arrangement was always credited to the Heartbreakers generally. *Long After Dark* garnered Campbell the most cowriter credits he'd had on any one album up to that point—four out of the ten songs—which also drives home the extent to which Petty was abdicating creative control of this album to his two most trusted band members. For "A Wasted Life," Petty said, "We just played it once, with Benmont out front." "Between Two Worlds" also opens with the piano forward. Petty even ended up composing "We Stand a Chance" on piano instead of guitar, though in his frantic effort to steer the record he insulted the pianist by adding a Prophet-5 synthesizer. "Benmont was really angry about the synthesizer," recalled Petty. "It was one of the only times we've used a synthesizer. He didn't want to do it."

For "Straight Into Darkness," Petty said, "I remember it really came to life when we turned it over to the piano. We let the piano take it." Of the intro, he recalled, "We were trying to do it more guitar-based, when we first started recording it. When it got turned over to the piano is when it really started to show what it was about. . . . Sometimes the songs won't reveal themselves to you until you find the right sounds and the right recording of it. And that was one like that. You couldn't really get everybody grooving the same way until we went over to the piano, and then everybody instinctually found what to play."

Petty concluded that "Straight Into Darkness" shows what it means to be "working with a group." The song is a testament to the marriage of the band, how its members rely upon each other when one of them is weak or when the situation is murky, how they go into things together. The intro is let to breathe for a full thirty seconds, Tench dropping down on each key with determination and Lynch offering a light feather dusting of cymbals before the strings all begin their walk-ons. The guitars persist at the end of each line in shimmering sustains but continually make way in support of the keys during the lyrics, showing restrained agreement that the song shall have no spotlight hogs. There's a little space for Tench's further contemplation between the chorus and the second verse, foreshadowing that we will meet him again after we cross the bridge verse. Petty wails at 2:05 with 1:44 left to go, triggering the strings to once again back off and make way for Tench's thirty-two uncrowded solo beats. Rather than soloing in the jam band sense of needless and endless jazziness, Tench chooses mainly to repeat his intro in a slightly higher key, climbing up the scale toward a tone that is mildly more optimistic than when the song began. That hope feels tentative, but the resoluteness of his touch on the keys remains the same as in the opening bars. By the twenty or so seconds left at the end of the verses, Tench has become the core of a composition that no longer has a lead player, all instruments fading away together without trampling each other.

As a prime example of the band snatching victory from the jaws of defeat, "Straight Into Darkness" has always had an anthemic quality to me. An anthem is a song that celebrates, calls listeners to action, or expresses pride in a nation or a philosophy. It's usually got a quicker tempo than a ballad. A ballad tends to be slower, and also focused on romance or melodrama in storytelling. By these very general definitions, "Straight Into Darkness" seems to be both an anthem and a ballad.

Is it possible for a song to be both a ballad and an anthem at once? Most people think of them as opposites. As Dave Marsh noted in comparing the Heartbreakers' two prior albums, "It's as if, on *Torpedoes*, all you could see was how much there was to win. On *Promises*, what you see is how much there is to lose." Cynthia Rose was more specific in the pages of *NME*: "Instead of finding glory in pure assertion, *Hard Promises* finds a dignity in acceptance." *Damn the Torpedoes* was full of anthems and glory, *Hard Promises* was full of ballads and acceptance. "As formidable a success as *Torpedoes* proved commercially," Rose continued, "its thinking suggested something beyond even the goods on display and *Hard Promises'* darkness on the edge develops, rather than merely continues, the story."

We can complicate the idea further by layering on the concept of a hit single. "In the past," noted biographer Nick Thomas, "Petty had been disappointed by his label's refusal to issue ballads as singles. Petty recalled, 'I don't think we had a hit ballad ever until 'Free Fallin'.'" Judging by the way they sung it out at shows—so loud and clear that Petty often conducted the audience instead of singing the chorus himself—lot of fans might classify "Free Fallin'" as an anthem rather than a ballad. If anyone could walk the line and capture both labels, it was Petty. As Zanes noted of his most famous composition, "With 'American Girl,' he brought home an anthem without having to dress it up in anthemic trappings."

I have listened to "Straight Into Darkness" hundreds of times with the specific intention of arranging it for myself to play. The easiest part of the song to hear is the way Tench drops down on the piano keys with a heavy hand, restraining his honky-tonk impulse from driving up the tempo, but still planting his fingers fully enough to prevent the notes from lingering in the air. When I play the song on a six-string banjo using nickel picks on two fingers along with the slide, it's Tench's contribution I naturally gravitate toward because each note is quite isolated and you get a decent jangle that way. But when I'm aiming to capture the resonance of the slide properly and let this tune drift and stretch a little further, my arrangement has more reliance on what I hear in the original guitar parts. This can be tricky because it's sometimes very hard to tell

Campbell and Petty apart when Tench is towing the rhythm line. The two guitars overlap and interweave into one harmonious, shimmering lead part, which may then have been multiplied by Iovine's insistence on tweaking through bits of many additional takes. Who knows how many tracks are embedded in the original studio recording of "Straight Into Darkness." This is not one of the many songs that any of the band members has ever classified as a one-take wonder. The guitar parts may be heavily cobbled together, and, as a consequence, it's not easy to arrange the song for a solo take on a slide guitar part.

There's an alternate studio version from 1982, found on the posthumously released *An American Treasure* box set in 2018, that is fully forty seconds longer than the one they ended up putting on the original album. It's not longer for any substantive reason, and they did right in choosing to use the other version on the album as a clearer representation of how the band could cooperate. Petty opens the recording by counting them in on a one, a two, a one, two, three, four. The arrangement features guitars that are less twinkly but further forward in the mix at the bridge and a longer, guitar-driven outro that ends with a hard stop instead of a simultaneous fade. There are a few extra seconds tacked on where somebody says, "That's pretty nice," to which Petty amusingly replies, "We got Iovine boppin'"—a small feat that was notoriously hard to accomplish at this juncture near the end of their production work together.

There's a concert version of "Straight Into Darkness" on *The Live Anthology*, released in 2006, which runs almost a minute longer than the studio recording. It falls as number eight of the fourteen tracks on disc one and was recorded in London at Wembley Arena on December 7, 1982. Must have been a great show, as two other tracks on *The Live Anthology* also appear on this four-disc set: a cover of Bobby Womack's "I'm in Love" and "Louisiana Rain," which was a Mudcrutch demo reworked to end up on *Damn the Torpedoes*. Petty always felt more able to put less popular songs in his English set lists. I couldn't find the complete list for the show on the 7th, but comparing the Netherlands set list from December 4 to the Scotland set list from December 9, the only change Petty made to the order of the first ten songs is to swap "Straight Into Darkness" with "You Got Lucky," bumping it from fourth to tenth. Maybe he moved it because he got what he needed from the song on December 7, or maybe he moved it because he didn't get what he needed. The extra minute the band took to play it revolved mainly around stretching out its silences, not jamming more effusively at the bridge or adding any solos.

There is video of "Straight Into Darkness" from the show in Germany on December 19, 1982. This version goes for an additional twenty seconds beyond what they played at Wembley two weeks before, and the visual elucidates which of the two guitarists played what part for the live arrangement. Petty held the rhythm and Campbell played lead, with Tench coming in slightly behind Petty on rhythm. When Campbell began a solo, Petty sidestepped behind him, moving over to stand next to Tench. Petty wiggled his shoulders and Tench bopped his head as they marked time together. As the piano prepared for the bridge verse, Petty stopped playing entirely to raise his hands in the air and exhort the audience to clap in time, which they did. The drums dropped away, ceding responsibility for the groove to audience and piano. Tench lobbed one bright and clear high note and Petty leaned away from the mic, nodded at him, and mouthed, "That's right," smiling. Then the redemptive lyric stepped to the forefront, gliding along on the twinkle of the piano. For the first two lines of the bridge verse, Petty still wasn't playing but instead motioned to the audience to carry on clapping, which they did. He resumed playing rhythm guitar when he began to sing the main point, that "Real love is a man's salvation."

By the time of their Farm Aid gig in 1985, the Heartbreakers could draw out the song to 4:47 only by borrowing a saxophone player and some maracas from others at the festival to offer a more traditionally expected method for the solo. During the sax bit, Petty wanders around onstage listening to it, but it's clearly not adding to the band's cohesion and they're all sort of biding their time until the sax goes quiet. The extra instrument feels among them but not of them, so they circle around it and allow it into their orbit more than truly welcoming and melding with it. Dylan saw them at that festival but did not play on the song. When he did play on it, during the 1986 True Confessions Tour with the Australian gigs available on the *Across the Borderline* album, the song could stretch as far as 5:14 due to Dylan pushing their three guitars forward at the bridge and the end, showcasing a philosophy about leading a band that was more in line with the 1982 alternate studio take than the route the band usually preferred to go. Dylan fits in better than a saxophone did because the Heartbreakers obviously love and respect him, feelings that help them to mindfully loosen every joint in the song in keeping with Dylan's interest in improvising. But the overall effect on the composition is that it begins to wander from its cohesive, equitable melody as Dylan tugs it into discordant territories that infringe on the slight momentum built by an audience keeping good time with hand claps a few moments before the band gifts Dylan free rein to do what he does.

The variety of runtimes for live performances of the song are otherwise seldom illuminating because there are many parts of its concert composition where at least one instrument has not much to do. The band filled this empty space with personal interactions onstage, as well as used it to bring in audience participation. Though the silence said it's a ballad, the energy moving between the band members and the crowd was more akin to what's expected from an anthem. The drummer was barely there. The guitars went in and out. Tench swiveled between four sets of keyboards to meet the needs of the live arrangement. For such an allegedly quiet song, it's pretty complicated to pick out the parts by ear alone.

Still, "Straight Into Darkness" is too impactful on me for me to quit trying my own hand at it. I guess mainly I try to privilege the vocals over the strings and give the notes that sustained shimmer. The G note in both chorus and verse can ring on and on for days because I play in open G tuning. Just zoom that slide right up off the fretboard and the note goes from a dirty insistence to a melodic scintillation that lilts away into fuzz, just in time for the next note to clamp down on the back end of it, always a D note whether chorus or verse. In order to let the hum linger as long as possible, I end up having to slow down the tempo even further into the territory of a ballad. According to the few live recordings, the Heartbreakers repeatedly did this, too. This is in spite of my natural punk tendency to speed up most songs into some kind of an exaggeratedly monstrous wrist- and elbow-tension experiment à la the Ramones, and despite the fact that "Straight Into Darkness" is my personal anthem.

The song is both a ballad and an anthem at once, even though that poses a paradox. Its composition has the twinkle of confused longing, which I arrange to play as a howling search of dark terrain. The way the Heartbreakers play it is terrific. My way doesn't really sound overmuch the same theirs, but it's as loaded with meaning as one musician with one voice can get and the original messages definitely do come through. It works for me. Said Petty, "That's the kind of band we are. If you let us have our way, sometimes we can just stumble into something great."

Song Lyrics

Verse 1

There was a little girl, I used to know her
I still think about her, time to time
There was a moment when I really loved her
Then one day the feeling just died

The first verse of "Straight Into Darkness" is about a relationship that sours. As guitarist Mike Campbell said of his songwriting partner, "There's times I'll hear a line and I'll think, 'He must be writing about Jane, or somebody.' But you can never really tell. We've all been hurt, you know. Tom doesn't write 'Good Day Sunshine.'" This personalization of universal hurt was Petty's working mode for the first half dozen albums, until around *Full Moon Fever*, when he realized he could use personas: "It was kind of like a bolt of lightning to my head, that it didn't have to be me, that I could assume characters."

Who is the little girl in line one? He used to know her, but still thinks about her occasionally or perhaps more frequently than that. Exactly how often is "from time to time"? Lines two and three contain vague suggestions of timing. He "really loved her"—for "a moment." "The feeling just died"—it happened "one day." One day, when? Why? It just happened. This is a classic story where the particulars of the person or the circumstance do not convey as much emotion as the waxing and waning of time. Said Petty, "I'm real good with ambiguity. You've only got four minutes or so in a song. If you nail things down too much, it doesn't seem to hold up to repeated listenings. You wear out on it quicker if you get a narrative song and you stay with the storyline really close."

This verse is like a little movie—the whole arc of the plot is paced out for us and we can see whatever detail we want to see there on top of it. All Petty maps out is the tick tock and his own agency in the situation. He doesn't speculate about whether the girl thinks of him, whether she really loved him back, or whether her own feelings similarly died. In a way, the omitted details blunt the true hurt of the verse. Petty doesn't dare speak for the girl's feelings or whatever became of her. He simply wonders alongside us, floating the prospect of the girl in a mystery space.

Unlike many rock stars, Petty's lyrical choices have almost always been kind to their female characters in this way. It doesn't matter whether he is writing in an expressly female persona, or in ballad duets like "Stop Draggin' My Heart Around," or in a male voice reflecting on his encounters with women. Petty has always been quietly but staunchly feminist. His own judgment about this was, "I was always the man who loved women. Not in a lascivious way. I grew up surrounded by women more than males. . . . And somehow I came out of it respecting women in kind of an equal way."

There's an obvious rhetorical difference in referring to a female as a "girl" instead of as a "woman," especially given the additional, lone qualifier that this girl is little. *Long After Dark* was Petty's fifth album, and we can count the number of references to girls in the other four. On the first album, there are eight mentions of girls, including a little girl in "Hometown Blues" and, of course, the titular "American Girl": "The 'American Girl' is just one example of this character I write about a lot—the small-town kid who knows there's more out there for them but gets fucked up trying to find it. Like the songs says, she was raised on promises. I've always felt sympathetic towards her." The American Girl is not little herself, but she did suspect there was a little more to life, and she had one little promise to keep. There's also a woman on the album, witness to the racist clash in "Strangered In The Night."

There are no mentions of women on the second album, but the one girl in "Listen to Her Heart" is perfectly capable of making her own life choices. On *Damn the Torpedoes* there are two women. The defects of the woman complained about in "Don't Do Me Like That" do not face Petty's judgment but rather that of his friend's. The woman Petty does complain about in "What Are You Doin' In My Life?" is not acting her age because she is stalking the singer like a crazed, teenage groupie. There are seven girls on the album: three mentions of one girl as the calming influence in "Here Comes My Girl" and three generic, plastic mentions peopling the satire of "Century City." Most interesting is the one mention in "What Are You Doin' In My Life?" of a girlfriend who is naturally disapproving of the stalker. Petty made three albums in the seventies where girls are sympathetic characters and women are not—and so there are very few women because Petty would rather say nice things about girls. Girls are tough and lovingly sensible in Petty's view, whereas women are capricious and comparatively insensible.

In Petty's lyrics there is no regard for age, no presumption of a correlation between age and innocence, and no particular interest in assigning a high value to innocence itself. To call an adult female a girl is not diminutive, and conversely, to call a young female a woman is not superlative. This preference for connoting superiority by means of a youthful designation also holds true for men and boys, where the fourth line of the second verse in "Straight Into Darkness" uses "man" as a derogatory exclamation of fear and suspense when "boy" could arguably convey the same message. The bright, strong females who make good decisions and maintain healthy relationships are the ones he calls "girls," while females full of fickle silliness or who are liable to mistreat their romances are called "women."

On the 1981 *Hard Promises* album immediately preceding *Long After Dark*, there are eight mentions of women to support the notion that "girl" is a preferential label. The women in "The Waiting" are ones to chase around, not dates to take seriously. Then there's "A Woman In Love (It's Not Me)," who's foolishly going to get her heart broken to pieces when she could've had everything the singer offered her instead.

There are three girls on the album: one fun-loving oddball type in "Kings Road," one worth fighting for in "You Can Still Change Your Mind." And a third is the self-respecting girl who bailed out in "The Criminal Kind," which deserves deeper scrutiny.

The second-to-last verse of "The Criminal Kind" is a precise parallel to the first verse of "Straight Into Darkness." It tells the same story in four lines with only slightly more detail and a dose of the girl's perspective, and it uses the same focus on timing. The first lines of each verse are only a syllable apart: "Yeah, and that little girl you used to know" is replaced by "There was a little girl, I used to know her." That lapse in their relationship is tossed off with the placement of "just," moving the word from the second line in "The Criminal Kind" to the fourth in "Straight Into Darkness." She "just doesn't come around." Since when? Unknown, just "no more." The "now" in the third line of this verse becomes "a moment" in that third line one album later. We know from the fourth line that she doesn't want to die in a liquor store, whereas on the next album's fourth line it's only her feelings that died.

"Died" is a monosyllabic word, unless you're composing a song. For "Straight Into Darkness," Petty draws it out to two syllables so that lines two and four are each nine beats. This is an example of how Petty began to tighten up his sense of lyrical meter between *Hard Promises* and *Long After Dark*. Whereas on "The Criminal Kind" he was content to have an odd number of verses and allowed this particular verse to go for a jagged 10-7-8-10 beats per line, the parallel verse from "Straight Into Darkness" keeps a steady 11-9-11-9. The rhyme scheme becomes similarly slick. In "The Criminal Kind," Petty is throwing out the slant rhyme of "know" with "more" / "store / "door" that relies upon dropping the R with his southern drawl to fit the words together. One album later, he gets more sophisticated, evading the problem of rhyming "know" / "loved" in lines one and three by ending both lines in "her," as well as adding a more classic slant rhyme of "time" / "died" that relies only on emphasizing the vowel sound instead of artificially siphoning out consonants by laying on a heavier Gainesville accent.

The girl in "The Criminal Kind" is not really a girl, either—she's a stand-in for the poor treatment of Vietnam veterans "who had been back for quite awhile, but they got no respect at all. And I had been reading this thing about how they had been shoved over to one side. Agent Orange had made them all sick, and the veterans' hospitals weren't treating them." So vets were being labeled as "the criminal kind," but Petty's use of ambiguity allows the label to attach itself to the government who shirked responsibility for supporting those who had fought its wars. The first verse of "Straight Into Darkness" might not be all that literally about a girl either. Real love comes in many less romantic forms, including the bond of a band, which is what Petty turns to in the second verse.

Verse 2

I remember flying out to London
I remember the feeling at the time
Out the window of the 747
Man there was nothin', only black sky

The second verse of "Straight Into Darkness" tells a more specific story than the first verse and also inverts its structure. Whereas the first verse puts imagery in lines one and two and the speaker's attitude toward the imagery in lines three and four, this second verse begins with the feelings and concludes with the image. This verse describes a trip abroad and showcases the vision of nothingness outside an airplane's window. The first verse gives specificity to the feelings, tracking their change over time, and characterizing their phases as real love that eventually died. By contrast, the feelings of the second verse are vague. We don't know what "the feeling" was, only that it is associated with London and the view from the plane.

In the early eighties, Petty wrote a great deal of lyrics directly concerning "feeling." The *Hard Promises* album contains a whopping fourteen mentions of "feel" or "feeling" across six of the album's ten songs. On *Hard Promises*, these feelings include a variety of both positive and negative associations: "heaven," "tonight might never be again," "good," "right now," "Sunday," "June," "different," "the danger," "guilty," and then the refrain on the last track reminds us that feelings can change. *Hard Promises* has as many mentions of "feelings" as Petty's first three albums combined, so it represents a significant increase in his explicit focus on feeling. *Long After Dark* contains seven mentions beyond the two in "Straight Into Darkness," but they are exclusively negative: "far away," "incomplete," "just can't understand," "each day going by," "dirty," "a little used up," and "let down." It's fair to say that Petty's main feeling at the time of *Long After Dark* was one of searching disappointment.

But this is not the feeling he associates with flying out to London. This verse is plainly autobiographical. As opposed to the "time to time" generality of the first verse, this verse takes place "at the time" that is well known to Heartbreakers fans as the time of the band's first major success. With their debut album and promotional tour in 1977, they hit it big in England long before getting any real traction in the United States. This would cement Petty's personal good vibes toward the country that had long been his main source of inspiration and fascination.

Common lore is that a meeting with Elvis propelled ten-year-old Petty into his musical career, but Petty draws a distinction between beginning to love rock and roll versus feeling called to pick up a guitar. He didn't pick up the guitar until he discovered the Beatles. He acknowledged, "England has always been Mecca to me," and called it "the home of our heroes." This is the source of Petty's preference for tight three-minute songs with shorter guitar solos, as opposed to the loose jams that proliferated like weeds among the southern rock groups prevalent during Petty's early days gigging in Gainesville. When Mudcrutch dutifully went up to Macon, Georgia, to seek out a deal with Phil Walden's Capricorn Records that would put them on a roster alongside the Allman Brothers Band and the Marshall Tucker Band, Petty reported, "We sat around all day and waited for someone to listen to our tape. And the answer was, 'It's too British. It sounds too English.' So we decided we were going to California."

In California, their English sound was met with an instant offer from the American arm of London Records. Petty returned to Florida to assemble his troops, only to receive a call from another interested Englishman. Denny Cordell swiped Mudcrutch out from under London

Records by intercepting them in Tulsa for casual studio hours. In Oklahoma, "it was just a windstorm of dust blowing everywhere and through the clouds, almost, this Englishman stepped through, who was really something to see. He had an earring, which you didn't see a lot of then, and a bandana. We had never met anybody that was English." If the band didn't feel good about the results, they could go onward to Los Angeles to sign up with London Records. Petty stuck with the charismatic Cordell instead, and, after rejiggering the lineup from Mudcrutch to the Heartbreakers, they cut the debut album.

It hit England like a bolt of lightning, and they got on a plane to support it: "It was an amazing time. Nothing will ever again feel like it did when it first started to happen. Nothing." On their first tour through the UK, they were opening for Nils Lofgren. Petty recalled that "there were riots fifteen minutes into the first gig. It's an incredible high—you're scared, you're excited, and you're pleased. . . . We'd never had people on stage knocking kids back down, and the girls breaking through." They got the front cover of *Melody Maker*, who declared them "one of the most in-demand bands currently playing this country." Manager Tony Dimitriades immediately rebooked them to headline the same venues they'd opened in for Lofgren. The album peaked at number twenty-four on the British charts with both "American Girl" and "Anything That's Rock 'N' Roll" in the British Top 40. The latter became such a popular British anthem that it was included on the European version of the band's greatest hits album decades later.

Benmont Tench agreed that "the UK seemed to get us immediately, even more than the Americans." Their debut album floundered in America for nearly a year, and the band came home to no fanfare whatsoever: "By the time we left England, we were a headlining band, and then we flew home and got off the plane, and you're nothing again," Petty said. He concluded that "Of everything we've done, that '77 tour was the most memorable: just the greatest time I ever had. It was like a rock 'n' roll dream, because we weren't of any significance in America yet, and our album had failed to sell at all. We probably would've been dropped [by Shelter] if it hadn't been for what happened in England. We did *Top of the Pops*, we had a record going up the charts and it was unreal. Our faces were on the covers of these weeklies, and the gigs were just fantastic."

For the band's second album, Petty was already trying to get ELO's Jeff Lynne to produce them, but the Englishman wouldn't sign on for that until a few albums down the road. On *Hard Promises*, Petty wrote "Kings Road" as an homage to his bewildered excitement about the London scene. His uncertainty about how to innovate their sound for *Long After Dark* clearly haunted him, and the "Straight Into Darkness" lyrics reflect that by turning once again toward the fond memories of their past London success. When the Long After Dark Tour was finished, Petty spent some time in his native South, but then went back for a stretch of vacation in England.

In fact, he was thinking about relocating the band to London and discussed it openly during the tour:

> LA is not nearly as bad a place as it's portrayed, but I don't think it's really the ideal place for us to continue right now. I don't think it would be a bad idea for us to get out of there for a while. . . . The English stuff seems a little more interesting to me right now. We used to spend a lot of time in London in the old days when we first started. It was really the first place we had success at all. I wouldn't mind going back to stay in London, if I could convince the band to go. I wouldn't mind taking on a different atmosphere because once you've had a group for seven years you've got to be a little aware about shaking them up from time to time.

His personal assessment of how *Long After Dark* had failed left him desperate for any kind of big change: "I think with the last record, I've refined that sound as far as I care to for the moment. So I think I'd like to strike out in some different direction just for my own amusement." He'd spent too long on the same set of ideas and felt the clock ticking. The first verse of "Straight Into Darkness" rhymes "time" with "died." The second verse rhymes "time" with "sky." He even draws out the phrasing into two beats just as he did at the end of the first verse, tightening up even further from the 11-9-11-9 meter of the first verse to 10-10-12-10 here. Though "sky" is a more optimistic association, to be sure, "sky" and "death" offer a parallel sense of hovering in uncertainty. The sky and death are always present, yet they are each a kind of dimensionless abyss.

From California, you've got to get on an airplane to go to London. Leaving aside that symbolic location of their success, Petty's lyrics have often shown an interest in the sky and flying. That plane in line three is what provides structure and direction to the limitlessness of the sky. Petty stated specifically that it was a 747. This detail may well be factual, but this jumbo jet is perhaps the readily available airplane model in the minds of most people, and it has garnered its fair share of references in songs that Petty would've heard before he wrote one into "Straight Into Darkness." Roger McGuinn put a 747 in "Draggin'" on his self-titled debut album in 1973. This is most notable, because Petty's work is so very often compared to his. The Hollies also mentioned one on "Mexico Gold" in 1974. Petty often covered McGuinn's "So You Wanna Be A Rock 'N' Roll Star" and so did Nazareth, who did a mash-up with it called "Telegram" in 1976 that included a 747 reference in the first of its four parts. Kiss uses one in "Rockin' in the USA" on *Alive II*, the recording made in 1977 on their Rock & Roll Over Tour, during which the Heartbreakers once opened for them. Several English musicians in whom Petty took an interest were using 747 references as well: ELO in 1977 for "Night in the City," Nick Lowe in 1978 for "So It Goes," and the Kinks in 1979 for "A Gallon of Gas."

One other specific airplane model was referenced during the Heartbreakers' early years, on 1978's "Hurt," which Petty and Campbell wrote together. This time the plane is a DC-10, and it proves an ironic counterpoint to the 747 because, in "Hurt," though the speaker of the song sits alone in darkness, the speaker is very glad to be escaping his vague backstory as a jilted lover by heading back to California. Los Angeles may have been home, but Petty thought of London as the fountain of all rock and roll dreams, the location of his own initial achievements, and ultimately the place that could reinvigorate his band after the slog that was *Long After Dark*. He couldn't wait to get out of Los Angeles. The gratitude he felt for that DC-10 flight home had faded.

There are also a few mentions of "sky" or "flying" that don't include planes. On the debut album there are two mentions of sky with positive connotations. The kids in "Anything That's Rock 'N' Roll" rocked "til the sky went light" with the sunrise. Petty's lyrics for "Luna" were entirely improvised in a Tulsa church as a kind of prayer to the moon. In the moonlight of "Magnolia" on the second album, he has a one-night stand with a woman whose eyes are as black as the sky. After "Straight Into Darkness," subsequent albums brought the additional good vibes of "Free Fallin'" and "Learning to Fly," among others.

Flight can be an escape, but it is also a meditative state of suspension. Petty's skies are generally a spacious place of peace, of the great wide open and a full moon fever. But the blackness of the sky consumes everything in "Straight Into Darkness." In this second verse, the band was headed into a future of possible stardom at that moment, radically uncertain as to whether they had delivered the goods or not. Everything hinged on their London reception and the conviction that they could succeed. This mystified confidence drives the dualities of the chorus.

Chorus 1

We went straight into darkness
Out over the line
Yeah straight into darkness
Straight into night

The chorus of a song is generally its most instructive part because it repeats, but Petty often prefers to put his lessons in the bridge or final verse. And he was not fond of handing out advice anyway: "I'm certainly not trying to preach or tell anyone what's right or wrong. I see myself as an observer, a reporter. I try to use what's happened to me or people in my immediate vicinity—and the better I get at expressing that and getting it across, the more meaningful the tunes are to people." Indeed, the chorus of "Straight Into Darkness" at first appears to be mostly reportage.

As the chorus applies to the first verse, the love died out and the couple went into darkness by separating. The darkness in this case is sad, maybe even bad, but we don't really know what became of either person once they passed into that darkness. Applied to the second verse, the band gets on a plane to London and flies into the darkness not knowing whether rock stardom awaits them when they land. In retrospect, we know they were greeted as a wild success. That darkness in this case builds excitement, represents the space of the unknown. One verse depicts an unhappy ending and the other depicts a happy one, though the four lines that report these two endings are identical.

These stories of how a romance died and how a career was born seem at cross-purposes in their definitions of darkness. We're accustomed to analyzing darkness as a symbol of negativity. In the binary of dark / light, night / day, black / white, we almost always assign negative value to dark / night / black. Petty himself sometimes fell into this assumption, once understandably describing his divorce as "the darkest period of my life." But the chorus of "Straight Into Darkness" works to dismantle this negativity by sending all the characters into darkness, some of whom emerge happily and some of whom don't. The darkness of "Straight Into Darkness" is therefore more value neutral—only a space of the unknown.

Many people have anxiety about the unknown, but others find amusement in it. The shroud of mystery laid over one's future is a powerful idea and, moreover, it's an inevitable reality. It's the famous Schrödinger's cat situation: you put a cat in a box with a poison that occasionally activates randomly, and then you don't know whether the cat is alive or dead until you open the box. That box has darkness in it. The darkness is a paradox, a situation at cross-purposes with itself because, until you open that box, the cat is dead and alive at the same time. The cat being out of sight means in some ways that it's firmly in mind. Petty's mother passed away during the making of *Hard Promises*, about which he reflected, "You can file things like that way, but they're still working on you." We are tremendously influenced by our uncertainty.

The only other mention of darkness on this album is in the title itself. What does *Long After Dark* mean? It's a nice way to start a campfire story maybe. It does have a scary ring to it, but let's think about time. Once it's long after dark, we're headed for sunrise. "Long after dark" may mean we can already see the light. If you can have an "after dark," you can also have a "before." The title carries this implication of a cycle, which really only means lining up both parts of the paradox end to end in a circle in order to hold on to two contradictory ideas at once. Is it light out or is it night? It's both. It's long after dark.

Benmont Tench even noted this paradox applied to the album's cover art: "[The album] was very angry or dark. It's got a nice cheerful red cover and silver back where everybody looks like, 'Hey, we're a pop band.' But it wasn't. It's got a real good mood and it sounds like the way we sounded then. It doesn't sound tricked-up at all to me. *Hard Promises* sounds tricked-up." We'll return to his valuation of honest authenticity versus the tricked-up later, but note the tension in the way the album's artwork reveals as it conceals. Ultimately, out of the paradox of the unknown comes the surprise of our future.

Petty was struggling with the recording of *Long After Dark*, and the band sensed this aimlessness. The Heartbreakers were becoming frustrated and bored. They were pressured by the paradox of wanting to break new ground but also wanting the new album to be done quickly. As with any band or any life, the unknown would have to resolve itself simply through the passage of time. Petty said, "My feeling is that you'll never really know what a band is, what it can do, if it doesn't have time to reveal its identity. If you put a group of great players together who share a love for a particular kind of music and allow them to develop, something is going to happen. But you won't know what it is until you get there. The surprises have kept me deeply engaged."

Waiting for inspiration to strike, waiting for a target at which to aim the album, was indeed the hardest part of making *Long After Dark*. Petty was losing sight of his own lesson from "The Waiting": "It's about waiting for your dreams and not knowing if they will come true. I've always felt it was an optimistic song." To wait is optimistic. To not know is optimistic. To look toward the future is optimistic. Optimism is essentially the faith that there is something long after dark. Then, from time to time, you get to let that darkness out of the box and either that cat is dead or it isn't.

Even the meter of the chorus underscores Petty's fearful indeterminacy. Counting only the syllables in each line, the beat structure appears to be 7-5-6-4, which is downright erratic compared to the more predictable, even patterns of the verses. Petty's phrasing draws out one or two extra syllables in the verses, but it adds many more beats to the chorus. In line two, he gives at least two beats to the word "line." In line four, he does the same to "night." He even pulls extra syllables out of "straight" in lines one and three. Maybe the meter of the chorus is 8-6-6-6. Maybe it's 7-5-7-5. The phrasing is proof of how Petty strained and searched for some direction. He said, "Phrasing is really important. A phrase can really convey a certain amount of emotion. If you change the phrasing, you can sometimes lose the emotion. . . . I think phrasing is really important. And so is meter. That you sing in meter and time. And even the way you sustain a line, or clip a line, is gonna really have an emotional impact." The emotional impact supplied by the vagaries of his phrasing in the chorus corroborates Petty's feelings at the time. He said, "If I don't believe it, I ain't singing it." He believed *Long After Dark* was on a wild goose chase, in pursuit of any sense of what his own expectations for it ought to be: "If there's one thing I know about music theory, it's that if you don't believe the singer, you won't believe the song." So he worried the album would fail because it only showcased his uncertainty.

No sense worrying too much over the prospect of a dead cat. Most things we worry about never happen anyway. Worry is an action, though, so at least we feel like we're doing something. Is optimism an action? How do we go into darkness? In the chorus, Petty says we go "straight" into it. This is a word he had never put in a lyric before. It has at least two possible meanings, and Petty was definitely messing around with that as he worked on this album. The evidence of this comes from Petty's reflection on its first track, "One Story Town," about which he remarked that the title was "kind of a play on words." It could either mean that the town's buildings are only one story tall, or it could mean that the town has only one story to tell.

The bulk of Petty's songwriting bears out this fondness for dualities, multiple meanings, and ambiguities. He considered these the essential tools of a lyricist. Later, when he completed "I Won't Back Down," this preference for a variety of available meanings initially left him horrified by what he'd written: "That song frightened me when I wrote it. I didn't embrace it at all. It's so obvious. God, there's nothing to hide behind. There's not a hint of metaphor in this thing. It's just blatantly straightforward. I thought it wasn't that good because it was so naked." He worried the song was too revealing, that it didn't employ any artistry of concealment, that it wasn't clothed well enough.

This leads to the most prominent and paradoxical meaning of "straight" in the chorus: to meet something head on, to go forward with honest authenticity. In this sense, Petty's never-ending train of successful legal battles against the recording industry and his general demeanor at all times will be enough evidence to confirm that he is one of the straightest-shooting rock stars. He said, "We've probably been the most successful underdogs in this business, and I still feel we're underdogs."

In interviews and in court, Petty plainly speaks whatever is on his mind to the point of a consistent, inadvertent insolence. Yet, in lyrics, he intentionally blurs meaning while expecting that the total package of the song will then speak straight: "I'm not one of those people who says, 'I just wrote a song about this or that subject.' Usually, when somebody says that, it's a bad song. I'm really wary of anyone who discusses their writing with me or tells me they wrote about this or that. That should be apparent when I hear the song, rather than them trying to help me out."

He respects the strategy of concealing to reveal, letting the cat be dead and alive simultaneously until the surprise. Embrace of this paradox is a philosophy of his craft, but also of his life: "That's kinda my theory of life—I'm just trying to go with it wherever it takes me and trying to be as honest as I can be with people." One need not jettison metaphor, ambiguity, or artistry in order to be honest. Petty's creativity, his very ability to forge concealments and mysteries, is after all his most organic instinct. It's the flow most natural to him—a flow with which he must go. This often requires a sense of humor.

People who can't go with the flow in life, people with no sense of humor, are uptight. This is the other meaning of "straight." It's normative and not at all queer. When Petty picked up jobs beyond his music gigs in high school and later when he was a groundskeeper at the University of Florida, he referred to these types of employment as "straight jobs."

A classic form of comedic dialogue involves a jokester and the "straight man," the former quite lively and the latter deadpan. If we take "straight" to mean "upright" and "uptight," that's a form of "straight" to which Petty is clearly opposed. He deviated from social norms, cooped up in his room with his record player, and even speculated that his parents were afraid he was gay.

Petty wasn't content with a "straight" life, but many people believe the surest route through darkness is the most prosaic—the straightest. When facing the unknown, citizen, just keep on the path set before you. This is akin to Johnny Cash's message in "I Walk the Line": reveal your straight and narrow road in order to conceal how much anxiety you have about the unknown. It's the opposite of a songwriter's impulse of concealing to reveal. "Straight" people suffer in their struggle to abide all the surprises and spontaneities of life.

In contrast to Cash walking the straight line, Petty sings that he will go "out over the line" because the future inevitably arrives, is ultimately revealed, is necessarily surprising. He was personally working on that fact: "I'm trying to learn not to resist change and accept that life is just a spontaneous chain of events. I'm not particularly accomplished at it, but I'm trying to go with the flow, because things are gonna change." Cash ultimately did approve of Petty's effort to go with the flow, and once gave him a birthday card inscribed, "You're a good man to ride the river with."

Moreover, Petty viewed this effort as his primary managerial responsibility to the Heartbreakers: "Me? I like whatever approach results in a great record. I don't care. I'll swim the English Channel if I have to. Whatever you want me to do. I just want to make the record in the way that I think is best in the moment. As I said, my job has often been to navigate through other people's resistance to change. . . . If we don't evolve, everyone suffers, particularly the ones—ironically enough—who are most opposed to those changes taking place." Resistance to change is futile. Might as well take uncertainty head on. Where there is darkness, best to go straight into it.

After you go into darkness, though, for a while, you're just still in it. Prepositions matter in this chorus. Petty doesn't say we go "with" darkness. He doesn't say we go "across" it. We don't go "over" it, "around" it, "near" it, "past" it, "under" it, or approach it any other way. We go "into" it. And we go "out over" the line. These are crossings where the end, the boundary, the horizon are not in sight. No guarantees about the future except the one implied by "after" in the album title. Finding one's way—beyond, through, out, apart from, despite, above, without, et cetera—to something that isn't darkness involves struggle. But hey, "There is a certain satisfaction in struggling for something and getting it. That's the American way."

When it came to working on *Long After Dark*, Petty forgot that struggle and satisfaction were two sides of one coin:

> When I hear *Long After Dark* now, I say, "This is great! Why was I so down on it?" It's just a record of pop songs, but I was feeling pressure, people saying that, "You didn't send us a message!" Well, I didn't have any message to send. That's a hard expectation to live with; it's flattering in one way, but I've never been able to look at myself well in that light. I get too self-conscious. It's hard to complain—what you're really striving for is to inspire someone. But it does seem in the last few years that's a certain great expectation of us and that can cause a certain amount of pressure.

On *Long After Dark*, Petty felt he had no message to send. That there is the key to the whole ball of wax. That album was the uncertainty that he went straight into, and he got uptight about the pressure of not knowing what it should be, what message he should send. Ultimately, he made a technically proficient album that did little more than report on the Heartbreakers feeling stuck in a rut. The band was boxed in, and fans listened to *Long After Dark* unsure of whether the band was alive or dead.

The whole album describes unresolved spaces: a town may have just one lame story; good love is hard to find; please deliver me; you can have a change of heart; we're only beginning to find things out; we stand a chance but it might be the same old you; don't waste your life. *Long After Dark* is one long description of a suspended state. It's the ultimate human paradox of knowing that we just don't know much. The album is an impassioned plea for guidance, but the message is not yet received. All Petty is sure of at this moment is simply that uncertainty exists. Ironically, this is the message that the chorus of "Straight Into Darkness" posits.

Bridge Verse

Oh give it up to me I need it
Girl, I know a good thing when I see it
Baby wrong or right I mean it

The bridge verse of "Straight Into Darkness" has three lines instead of four: "We always call it 'verse, bridge, chorus.' 'Bridge' is something that's a departure," said Petty. He considered lyrics over the bridge to be like a turn or a volta in a Shakespearean sonnet: "It's the part of the tune where you go somewhere else. . . . It's almost like the narrator drifts off into a place of very high, even mystical emotion. It provides a kind of road sign to that last, very personal verse." After one minute and forty-three seconds, with two minutes left to go, the song's apex of vehement pleading arrives.

Petty's entreaty to "give it up to" him has neither subject nor specific object. Not only do we not know what the "it" is that should be given up to him, we don't even know who is supposed to give it up. Line two addresses a girl, perhaps from the first verse or at least harkening back to that. Line two clarifies that "it" is a "good thing." We do know this good thing arrives via another person. The lost love in the first verse takes place between two people. The musical success of the second verse is shared by all the Heartbreakers. So whatever this good thing is, seems like we don't encounter it alone.

The third line raises the stakes by removing that good thing from the value judgments of right and wrong. The speaker doesn't care if he's right or wrong about it, instead focusing on the fact that he "means" it, that this good thing must be given up to him. Once again, there is effort to eschew preaching and just report the speaker's needs or feelings. "Good" has appeared regularly in Petty's lyrics in a positive context relevant to philosophizing on how life should be, as opposed to other simple uses like "goodbye." It turns up on average three or four times per album until *Long After Dark*, on which "good" is used five times. Nor is his usage of "right" very statistically significant. That one also shows up an average of three or four times per album, then three times on *Long After Dark*.

It's a different story with his usage of "wrong." Until *Hard Promises*, Petty had never written "wrong" in a lyric. In 1981, it showed up on "Nightwatchman," where the guard on his door is shooting the breeze in a series of blustery throwaways. After that lone mention across four albums, *Long After Dark* uses "wrong" in three separate songs that occur in sequence on the album. "Finding Out" opens with the warning that something is wrong with the speaker's loneliness, but he doesn't know exactly what yet. He suspects he needs to fall in love. On "We Stand a Chance," the first song on side two, the speaker acknowledges he might be wrong about a love affair. What do these two lovers stand a chance of? The very same "real love" that died in the first verse of "Straight Into Darkness" and that will return in its fourth verse.

Taken together, these three songs describe the cycle of a romance: he gets pulled into it, thinks it might be the real thing, but then it fades. Petty doesn't know how to define what he is looking for, but he'll know it when he sees it, and the main thing is simply that he still wants it. His plaintive wail insists that this real love must be out there somewhere, and, on the bridge, Petty lets his vocals go into a raw whine: "The thing about vocals, the only thing about vocals for me is believability, it's not about being in tune or hitting a note, it's not about anything except making people believe what you're singing." The emotion of the bridge on "Straight Into Darkness" is clear and convincing, but Petty would move from believability to explicit statements of belief for his final verse.

Verse 4

I don't believe the good times are over
I don't believe the thrill is all gone
Real love is a man's salvation
The weak ones fall the strong carry on

Of the first line in the last verse of "Straight Into Darkness," Petty said, "I thought it was a nice optimistic verse in the end: 'I don't believe the good times are over.' I was probably feeling a little melancholy around that time." In preparing to analyze this verse, I was surprised and horrified to find that the band's official website butchered it in two places. Most ironically, the site had completely left out the line to which Petty attributes the song's optimism. It's just not there—an oversight that proliferates widely across accounts of this song's lyrics online, alongside the other offense. Less ironic but more irritating to this English teacher, the last line of the verse includes a homophonic misspelling of "weak" as "week." If ever the band's webmaster rectifies these, it'll be the surest proof I made a difference in this world.

The first two lines of the verse begin "I don't believe." Anaphora, where two or more lines of a verse begin with the same word or phrase in a row, is commonly used in Petty's work: four times in 1976, three times in 1978, three times in 1979, then six times each on *Hard Promises* and *Long After Dark*. All but one of these albums has ten songs on it, so Petty uses anaphora on 30 to 60 percent of his songs. Generally, the merit of this literary device is that it gives emphasis through repetition, often with some kind of a slight turn or surprise variation that makes the ends of those lines particularly meaningful. He could tell us what he believes but chose instead to tell us what he doesn't believe.

For a songwriter who claims to prefer reportage to preaching, Petty sure relies heavily on "don't" in his lyrics. The word is a command. "Do not" is inherently prohibitive. He used it thirty-two times in 1976, fifteen times in 1978, fifty-two times in 1979, and thirty-one times on *Hard Promises*. That's an average of thirty-six times per album until *Long After Dark*, where Petty writes "don't" into his lyrics for a career low of just thirteen times. That's less than half his average usage, yet he works up dismay in these first two lines for good reason: it sounds sappy to affirm that one believes in the existence of good things and thrills.

From time to time, we all step into a darkness where it seems that good times may be over and thrills may be gone. So we don't need to affirm that they did exist in the past. Instead, we need to look toward the future in order to defeat our present uncertainty. Optimism in this case means issuing a denial. Good things and thrills may not be here in the darkness of now, but they're not over and gone. Petty doesn't believe they're through. The negation is more powerful than any affirmation of good things or thrills because it looks to the future instead of clinging to a lovely past that bears little resemblance to the dark present.

These thrilling feelings are located in both romantic and musical relationships. Though the word "thrill" itself doesn't appear in any lyrics except to ward off the stalker in "What Are You Doin' In My Life?," Petty is fond of using it in interviews. In characterizing the extent of his love for Jane Benyo in 1992, he said, "I'm still thrilled about her." When Emmylou Harris recorded a cover of "Thing About You" in 1985, Petty said it was "a real thrill." When Roger McGuinn got added as an opener for the Dylan tour and the Heartbreakers began backing him on Byrds songs, Petty called it a "great thrill." Playing on "Like a Rolling Stone" with Dylan was also "such a thrill." His ad-libbing of the "Swingin'" lyrics and getting it recorded as a one-take wonder was "really a thrill." Of his work on *Wildflowers*, he said, "Anytime you get to work with an orchestra, God, it's a thrill." He had been using this word to describe his feelings for people and bands across four decades.

In line three, he declares that these thrills come from a love that is real, that it exists and it is our salvation. The new presence of Howie Epstein would eventually illustrate this in an unusually tangible and poignant manner. It's common knowledge that the bassist died of heroin complications in 2003. Lesser known is that Epstein's dog died the day before he did. Benmont Tench confirmed the seriousness of Epstein's relationship with the dog: "It was the best look in the world. There's Howie, playing his bass and singing better harmonies than you ever heard in your life, and there's this giant dog at his feet, looking up at him with all the love in the world. I think Howie and Dingo were literally best friends."

Epstein officially joined the Heartbreakers in 1982 for the Long After Dark Tour, and the dog was born in 1987. In 1995, five tours later, when the dog was eight years old, Epstein requested and received his own tour bus, ostensibly so that he could more easily care for Dingo. The band saw much less of Epstein as a result, and, though his addiction would not overtake him for eight more years, the additional privacy no doubt allowed his drug abuse to escalate. In human years, Dingo was more than twice as old as Epstein when they both passed. Petty felt the deaths were connected: "[Howie] had him for years and years and years. He was very tight with the dog, he took him on tour with him, he wouldn't be apart from this dog. And I heard, through the grapevine, that he had broken up with Carlene [Carter], and that he was staying in New Mexico full-time. And the dog died. And the next day Howie died."

Petty understood a variety of bonds to be sacred like this. Dogs, guitars, band members, and lovers were all mystic parts of his family. He speculated that "maybe a man's king when he's fallen in love and raised a family. Maybe that's the greatest reward there is in life. And, strangely enough, available to everyone." Despite having already locked down that greatest reward, in writing *Long After Dark*, Petty was preoccupied by the idea of salvation in part because he was concerned with his own need to be saved from making a shoddy album. Though he had used versions of "save" in lyrics before, this album characterizes real love using language with more explicitly religious connotations, most obviously on "Deliver Me," where it's the answer to when our hearts can't understand.

The second verse of "We Stand a Chance" also uses anaphora for "God knows." Petty had used either "thank God" or "God damned" on his first three albums, as expressions of gratitude or condemnation, but this is the first time he used God as a description of knowing. People may have miscommunications or be uncertain, but Petty's assertion that God knows better buttresses the existence of love as real despite it having temporarily faded from human view. We inevitably sometimes enter into darkness, so salvation is needed not from the darkness but for us while we are in that darkness. If darkness is uncertainty, real love saves us in it because real love is a strong conviction. Real love is the opposite of uncertainty because it sets up something permanent against something temporary.

The sun will come up again and darkness will dissolve. The sun is there even when we don't see it. In line four, remembering this fact allows us to be strong and carry on. Petty was afraid that the album was weak and that it would fall, an uncertain terror magnified by his otherwise strong personal mojo. Always the underdog, losing or quitting were never options he allowed himself to seriously entertain. Even when tragedy struck and some lunatic burnt down his private residence, Petty went onward with determination: "I think I'm going to be alright," he told the press after the fire. "I'm the kind of person who presses on." He kept his eye on the future and just kept marching toward it. That's the action of optimism, and by omitting two words from the final chorus of "Straight Into Darkness," he would cement that optimism as a proper recommendation.

Chorus 2

Straight into darkness
Out over the line
Yeah straight into darkness
Straight into night

By eliminating two words from the first line of the "Straight Into Darkness" chorus during its final repetition, Petty does succeed in preaching. The first two verses end in a complete sentence, so that the chorus begins a new thought. In the fourth verse, however, Petty ends on a preposition. It could be interpreted as a complete sentence, except he then eliminates "we went" from the first line of the chorus, with the result that the chorus becomes a continuation of the thought in the fourth verse: "the strong carry on . . . straight into darkness."

Petty changed up the words of a chorus deliberately on some songs because "sometimes if you do that, it can give you a really nice build. Even a *slight* change can really lift things all of a sudden. It's a good thing. I wish I did it more often, now that you mention it. It's an old songwriter trick. But it will raise things up. It's almost like a key change." In this case, the two-word deletion changes both the subject who goes straight into darkness and the verb tense in which that action happens.

In the first two go arounds, the chorus says "we" went into darkness. For the first verse, this refers to the two people who were formerly in a relationship. In the second verse, it refers to the Heartbreakers who went to London together. The song builds from a consideration of two people to a half dozen people, and here at last, to include everyone. There are no more stories in the fourth verse, just archetypes of the weak and the strong and their epic, mythic salvation as they go straight into darkness armored by their real love. It gets beyond "we," to "all." As Petty previously noted, this solution of real love is strangely available to everyone. So there is an expansion of the subject to whom the chorus applies, and there's a corresponding explosion of the logistics. Eliminating "went" moves the action from the past tense into the future and maybe even the present.

Now and later, the strong carry on. It's the only authentic choice, no matter how uncertain that darkness gets. Petty often weighed the consequences of marching on, in his life and work alike, but found no alternative: "The guy in those songs *isn't* a loser. I've been through things where I thought it just couldn't get no bleaker. It was a bad stretch, but I had to bring myself out of it. If you can't take the attitude that even losers get lucky, I don't see how you can face life. I figure you either lose your girl or your job—sometimes both. But why let anyone know they've beat you?"

Paradoxically then, the strong bring themselves out of darkness by going straight into it because the only way out is through. The band knew it, too. When the Long After Dark Tour was over, Campbell recalled that "it was reaching a point where everyone was getting a bit stale with each other, inspirational-wise. We just weren't committed as a band," so they had a meeting. Petty said, "It took us all getting together in one place and saying, 'Well, do we break up?' and no-one wanted to." They would lead their fans by example.

"Straight Into Darkness" has often been mistaken by fans as a major bummer. At times, even the Heartbreakers seemed not to recognize the song's true message. But in the final analysis, they do manage to shake off uncertainty, circling back to a collective optimism and the necessity of pushing onward in life. Petty's ultimate judgment of the song more than twenty years later was that "there's some hope in it. It wasn't just a downer. [Laughs]." That bit of laugher, ten additional years later, is all the testimony we need to learn how Schrödinger's cat feels about having nine lives.

Handwriting

The day before I got on a plane to Red Rocks Amphitheater, Tom Petty's Twitter account posted a photo of the original handwritten lyrics for "Straight Into Darkness." An omen? Let's be careful not to assign too much intentionality to a rock star's official social media feed. It's likely that Petty never laid a hand on the account since its inception in 2008. Still, how many times has a photo of handwritten lyrics appeared on @tompetty before this instance? Three times out of nearly five thousand posts, and one of those three times was again the "Straight Into Darkness" lyrics in October 2015.

Those two other handwritten lyrics sheets were "Love Is a Long Road" in September 2015, and "Southern Accents" in April 2017. All the lyrics are torn out of either spiral-bound notebooks or top-stapled legal pads. Presumably there's easy access to a bunch of other lyrics in these same stacks of paper, yet none have been posted. Why these three songs, and why "Straight Into Darkness" twice? In 2015, the photo got 371 hearts, 114 retweets, and 25 comments. In 2017, the same photo got 470 hearts, 95 retweets, and 11 comments. Petty had over three hundred thousand followers on Twitter at that time.

The "Southern Accents" lyrics frankly don't look like Petty's handwriting, based on the dozen or so other samples of it out there. Yet this photo garnered 722 hearts, 123 retweets, and 38 comments. "Southern Accents" was of course the title track on the 1985 album. The "Love Is a Long Road" photo garnered 331 hearts, 123 retweets, and 20 comments. Of the twelve tracks on 1989's *Full Moon Fever*, five were hit singles, and "Love Is a Long Road" wasn't one of them. In 2015 and 2017 alike, "Straight Into Darkness" generated somewhat less social media attention than other songs even though the time period of the posts is reasonably similar.

I looked at those lyrics for a long time. Charmingly, Petty wrote his name at the top right corner, just like he probably did in school. Petty used a blue ink pen, and there's not one scratch-out until the bottom of the page, where he appeared to want to squeeze in a verse but ultimately decided to cross it all out and give it room to breathe on the back side of the paper instead. In the blank line between verses, he wrote in parenthetically "continued on back of this page." No kidding, you can see right through to it with the paper so thin and the ink bleeding so thick. The result is a layered look. You can also see what he'd put on the previous page. It's "The Same Old You," a Petty/Campbell collaboration that appears directly after "Straight Into Darkness" on the album. The ends of several of its verses are plain as day, not facing backward, on the handwritten sheet: "politician" and then a little lower, "Cadillac," "back," and "America."

As a teacher, I've developed a pretty fine sense of what means what when it comes to handwriting. Petty's handwriting looks a good deal like my maternal grandmother's. She wrote me a letter a week my first year of college, and not holding on to those is one of my few regrets in this life. Lulu and Petty share a disdain for proper capitalization, working more by instinct than by the rules. Sometimes Petty would use a front cap to begin a new line, and sometimes not. Sometimes he'd capitalize an *N* in the middle of a word and sometimes not. The *R*, *A*, and *F* were always capped throughout. The caps themselves were the same size as his lower-case lettering, which is a mark of humility. His *G* and *Y* hung down off the line without hooking, proof of a mind that is already looking ahead to the next letter. The *J* had a hook, but it's flat instead of curved, coming out at a sharp angle. Petty's handwriting had few curves and very many angles. His *S* was particularly jagged, with the *M* and *W* also quite pointy. This shows he's an ambitious sharpshooter, intelligent but aggressive, no dressing things up. He took the time to hang an apostrophe on nothin' and twice used long, straight dashes to indicate cutting away to the swell of the music. Petty dotted every *I* high above it, a tiny floating detail of imaginative control. He slanted words slightly right, which indicates he is sociable but not necessarily outgoing. The letters were smallish, focused, and precise, spaced close together but not sloppily connecting. His *E* was closed, no useless space, more skeptical than emotional. He had an extra-long cross on his *T*, and his own name at the top looked just like the writing on the rest of the page, no branding or calculating there, only determination maybe to the point of stubbornness. Even his choice of pen, his preference for that inky bleed, and no scratch-outs, says he's sure of himself, quietly committed. Petty was legible and comfortable.

All this we can infer from his music anyway. If I got handed these lyrics on the first day of school without getting to size up the one who wrote them and without regard for their content, I'd judge that here's a kid likely to end up with a B in my English class—intellectually capable of an A but too stubborn to follow enough instructions to get there and uncaring enough that he's liable to backslide into a C if I don't look out for him. And I would indeed look out for him, because there's something in the penmanship that hints he may be gifted in a way that grades can't reflect.

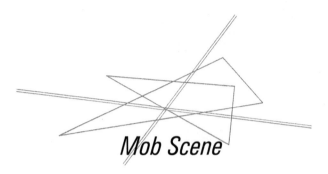

Mob Scene

Mine

It brought me a kind of peace to see the Heartbreakers live in concert as often as time and money would allow. A fundamental irony developed in my commitment to seeing these shows because of how frequently my experience of attending them had been plagued by some kind of violence.

At the first concert, we had lawn seats and brought my in-laws because they were determined to visit despite our plans to go to this concert. They consider themselves hip people and do tend to stay up late, so we used it as a bonding activity. My wife's family thinks of me as a stoic and a hard case, so they were psyched for the possibility of unobstructedly observing me continuously displaying joy for two or three hours. The lawn was on a bit of a sloping hill, like a natural riser, so everyone behind us was also slightly above us. Living in such close proximity to Gainesville, Petty's Atlanta shows were generally a mix of diehards like myself and classic rock fuddy-duddies. The younger part of the crowd skewed toward ball caps and frat boys, and a few of these less-than-interested dudes happened to be perched directly behind us on the lawn.

I say "perched" because their mostly empty beer cans repeatedly tumbled down onto our otherwise dry blanket at regular intervals throughout the show. When their sneakers also got a little too close, my in-laws started in with the stink eye, which, in their uncaring intoxication, the rowdy gentlemen behind us did not even perceive. Nor did they heed the escalation into hissing, so that finally my father-in-law swiveled around and started lecturing them. Their crabbiness became mildly threatening before tapering off into a "thanks, grandpa" dismissiveness as they shuffled off for greener pastures. It was a buzzkill, at best. At worst, I thankfully avoided laying hands on some drunken tomfools twice my size.

Another time on another lawn, I was there with my pal from grad school who's as big a Pettyhead as I am, plus my publisher and his best friend who loved the band but had never been to a show. We got tan and wasted on eight-dollar tallboys plus the tequila I smuggled through security in my boots, and it was a great time. Then, as we were all stumbling out into the starry night, a drove of satisfied customers shambling slowly toward the parking lot, one giant of a man holding his lawn blanket against his hulking chest galloped furiously against the current of the crowd as people parted to make way. He came up on us so fast that we hardly saw him before he reached us. He'd obviously left a human or an object on the lawn and was frantically trying to get back to whatever he lost. He did not care who was in his way, which, in this case, meant my poor publisher, who couldn't sidestep quick enough and was instantly bowled over straight backward into the arms of my other pal, who was herself then nearly knocked off balance.

The whole thing happened in a silent blink, and I spun around to inquire about next steps. I might want to knock his head off, if I could reach it, just to bring some sense of the calm of the present moment back into him. Might want to at least give a sort of "Hey, asshole" warning flag to the still-parting sea of people behind us. It seemed like a pretty impersonal affront and the guy was already fading fast toward the entry gates, so nothing happened. My publisher still makes jokes about how I failed to defend his honor. It was scary as hell for a split second, and the surprise of it still resonates. We can pretty well laugh about it now at a distance only because my publisher didn't crack his head open.

There's a buddy I often go to concerts with when my wife doesn't feel like tagging along. Twice, he's had to go to the emergency room the day before a concert. How many times has he been to the hospital in all the time I've known him? Just those two times. It's freaky. Every time we get some tickets, we crack jokes about what kind of accident might befall him on the eve on the show. The second time he bailed on was pretty special, because it was Mudcrutch. That's the original Gainesville project: Petty on bass, Campbell and Tench as ever, the brother of a guy from the Eagles on second guitar, a different drummer, and sometimes a banjo.

My grad school pal made the pilgrimage, and my buddy's ticket went to Abby, a best friend of mine who's good at making spontaneous plans. The show was at the Tabernacle, a Baptist church more than a hundred years old. Great acoustics. Our sixty bucks for general admission landed us in roughly the tenth row, where tickets for that seating at a larger Heartbreakers venue would easily run two hundred bucks. And who knew when Mudcrutch would rise again between the Heartbreakers' tours. This might have been our only chance to see them, ever. My pal and I were definitely going to our church that night, plus my pal was thinking about being a Methodist, and Abby's a real live Methodist, so we all took it as a divine intersection of the things we loved and needed.

It was mostly a great time. There was this family of six-footers right in front of us, which was hard. The mom arrived slurry and the dad was a world-class enabler. The son had on a ball cap and almost never put his phone away except to hug his girlfriend from time to time. But this was the kid's first Petty show, and the mom was going on and on about how she's seen him seventeen times. They annoyed the hell out of me, but I'll be damned if the mom didn't belt out every single song lyric correctly. Not just from the newest album and not just the hits; she really knew every word. So I had to forgive all of her brood's goings-on.

The violence came from elsewhere. Abby had been standing behind me to the right, getting elbowed by some woman next to her for a half hour or so, but since she has little kiddos and has taught teenagers for years, there isn't much that can throw her into conflict with other adults. Abby made the best of it, which annoyed this other woman all the more. So the woman then tried to get into it with my grad school pal, who is a conflict-averse Canadian librarian not interested to truck with any shenanigans at the show of a lifetime. As I increasingly noticed my two friends scooting closer into my own narrow personal space, I became aware of the fact that this woman was basically herding them toward me with her aggressive vibe.

You got to let that dark magic alone for as long as you can in hopes that it drifts away, and I did until she started flinging words. I guess she kept yelling at them "Three hours!" until they were visibly shaken. Being the boldest or at least the meanest of our trio, I stepped in to ask the woman if she was all right. Not rude, not accusatory, merely with a genuine interest in what the kerfuffle was with my friends. She just kept repeating "Three hours!" I asked if that was how long she had waited in line for the show, or how long she drove to get here, or whatever.

She said it was how long she'd been standing in that spot, at which point I woke up to several alarming facts simultaneously. One, the show had not been going on for anything nearing three hours yet. Two, the woman was standing in a spot that I had newly vacated perhaps ten minutes before as the crowd crushed ever closer toward the front of the stage. Three, her pupils were pinholes but she didn't smell like alcohol, which meant heavy drugs. Four, her boyfriend was making apology faces at me and attempting to bear hug her from behind as she got her elbows up to point a finger at my chest.

As this conflict was taking place, Petty was up there crooning "Crystal River" with its mantra of "nothing can touch me here, nothing can touch me here." The low volume of the refrain allowed me to hear perfectly when she spat "stupid cunt" at me. I am a lot of things, but I am not stupid. I was shocked and mildly afraid. More afraid than I've been of another human being in a long while. Not because of the C-bomb, which

I've been known to drop myself from time to time, but because she so badly wanted to throw a punch and was clearly blind with rage. It wasn't what she said, as much as the way she said it. The impersonal, irrational nature of it was scary.

There I was, just another Pettyhead with a little buzz, minding my own business at showtime, when this total stranger so radically misinterpreted my existence as a challenge of some incomprehensible kind. So I asked the boyfriend whether we were going to have a problem. Because I'd never been in a fistfight. I feel in my heart that I'm willing. But there was a good chance this woman's face would feel nothing, and she was a couple inches taller than me in addition to being squirrelly from some type of serious upper. If I'm going to get in a physical altercation, I'd like it to be over something substantive, and ideally I'd like to win. This was not a good fight, and my chances were less than even.

And if I'd been booted from my only opportunity to see Mudcrutch, I wouldn't forgive myself easily. Fortunately, the boyfriend was on equally high alert and doing his best to steer her toward the aisle by rocking gently out of time to the beat. By the end of the seven-minute jam we had two or three yards between us, which I guess was enough to get out of her blast radius. I watched her then cherry-pick similar trouble with a couple of other people before our three hours were up.

After "Crystal River," the band went into "Victim of Circumstance." I put my forehead to the forehead of my pal, and we had a shallow laugh with one eye still on the perimeter. A half hour before the random, manic incident with that stupid cunt, tears were silently rolling down my face as I thumped my chest to the chorus of my favorite song on Mudcrutch's new album, because I've had to fight every day of my life and it's a beautiful world.

I was always seeing Petty, as long as he came around. Didn't want to keep waiting for the other shoe to drop at those shows, but this did look like a real trend, and you just never knew what an audience would do. From the stage, they were preaching all this common sense about the merits of kindness, hope, and forgiveness. Couldn't always count on the congregation to receive it correctly, even when everybody there had bought a ticket to take what was ostensibly the same ride. I wondered about whether Petty worried over the occasional ugliness of his crowds, whether that dude swimming against the current ever found what he lost, whether that woman remembered us at all in the sober light of day, whether her boyfriend stuck around. But all that was unknowable to me. So I just got on the phone to see how my buddy was doing in the hospital, and he was going to be fine. We would all, individually, most likely be fine. How we would manage our experience collectively was a somewhat more dubious matter, but it didn't keep me from buying the tickets.

Theirs

When tallying up all the times one has closely witnessed or directly encountered violence at Tom Petty shows, naturally one begins to wonder where the fault lies. If you went into a room and it smelled like shit, so you left and went into another room that also smelled like shit, you'd check the soles of your own shoes. I wondered whether I was a magnet for these occurrences, but even the most cursory look at the Heartbreakers' concert history reveals it ain't me, babe. It's in the aura of the band.

The mob scene is largely what drew Petty to music in the first place. Before he ever dreamed of touching an instrument, he'd sit around in his room all day blasting records. His childhood encounter with Elvis had left a long shadow for reasons that had nothing to do with the music. As a boy, Petty hung out with his uncle, who was working on a film crew. Even though Elvis was past his heyday in the early sixties, Petty remembers that the presence of Elvis on the set of *Follow That Dream* generated "the biggest crowd I've ever seen in the streets of Ocala."

Even during the filming, what he remembered most vividly is the massive influence of the crowd: "We watched [Elvis] shoot this scene. Which was really funny, because every time he pulled up in the car, the crowd would break through the barricades and just charge him. So it took them hours just to shoot this little scene of him getting out of the car and walking in the door. Because they couldn't control the crowd; they were just insane." By the time his attention turned from Elvis on set to the Beatles on *Ed Sullivan*, this insanity was also gendered. Watching the Beatles on television, Petty was most impressed by "the girls screaming—I never seen or heard anything like that in my life. Girls were going insane, crying and waving. You just knew the TV studio was being turned upside down." Only then was he called to pick up an instrument himself.

He wanted in on that mob scene, to be a part of the forces that could generate it. When viewing it from the outside, he found massive crowd antics to be an amusement, a party, a way to get through to some ladies. Despite peripheral acknowledgments that the film crew was hindered in their work and the studio people were frazzled by all the fan wrangling, he still wanted to produce this experience by forming his own band. Indeed, Mudcrutch's rise to prominence in Gainesville in the early seventies resulted in over a thousand people attending the little festival they put together on their farm. It was big and rowdy enough that the property owner and the police warned them off of doing it again—orders they disobeyed twice.

Their regular gig at Dub's bar down the road was terminated after Tom Leadon got into a fight with the owner that also caused him to leave Mudcrutch. As Mudcrutch dissolved into a proto-Heartbreakers arrangement, Benmont Tench's arrival was like a lightning bolt: "I had a Wurlitzer with a Marshall stack. It was fantastic—100 watts of a Wurlitzer. It got loud. We played some high school auditorium and cracked the ceiling." That was Tench's very first gig with the band. The school threatened to sue for damages.

As fate would have it, Stan Lynch was in the audience for that show because it was a field trip for a rock music history class he was taking. The drummer was well known for being a hothead even then. Lynch himself admitted, "I used to get in fights with people I was in groups with all the time. . . . I'd get pissed off and go beat up the bass player." Petty agreed, "We butted heads a lot for twenty years. . . . We fought a lot. *Every*one fought with Stan, really." At some point after Lynch joined the Heartbreakers, Petty had to wag a finger at him about it: "Look man, you can call anybody anything you want . . . that they suck, and you can say it loud, but you can't lay a hand on anyone in this band."

In some ways this was the pot calling the kettle black, though Petty's driven intensity did not lead him to fistfights. After the band moved west and publicity started to pick up in England, Petty was comfortable easing into the tough-guy persona that sprung from a few leather jacket photo shoots and the market's failure to adequately categorize his genre of music. The jacket had some bullets on it. The band was slotted somewhere between punk and new wave. Petty kept his fists lowered, but there was a series of anecdotes about knives that still resonates.

As Courtney Love told journalist Jim DeRogatis, "I've heard this story about Tom Petty: When he was dealing with people, he'd take this knife and stab the desk when he wanted to make a point." In a tense meeting at ABC Records, Petty once resolved the impasse by producing a knife and admiring its blade. He once said on record with the British press, "Call me a punk again and I'll cut you." He was ironically deploying their image of him against them, but many didn't get the joke.

He also perpetuated versions of this joke onstage. In the autumn of 1977, when the band's debut album finally charted in the United States ten months after its initial release, the hit was "Breakdown." On the record, this song clocks in under three minutes. In concert, Petty would extend the jam on it, doubling the length of the song by acting out impromptu monologues where he underscored the attitude of frustration in his words by strangling his mic stand.

In the summer of 1978, the band returned to England, where the mob scene left them feeling unfulfilled. Of their Knebworth festival set, Petty reflected, "I really felt distant from 100,000 people." Days later at the Marquee Club in London, he passed out onstage due the intense heat created by overbooking the venue. Petty lamented, "We haven't played bars in awhile and I miss it. You can see everybody right there. I don't mind playing bars, they're fun." Already during his very first tour, the mob scene was starting to get to him.

When they returned to the United States in July, faulty wiring at a Miami show resulted in Petty getting electric shocked by his microphone. After briefly leaving the stage, he returned to finish the set but called off the next night's show in Dayton. Perhaps every band eventually faces these kinds of incidents. Set design is imperfect, props fail, pyrotechnical effects are tricky to control, and not every mic is properly grounded. Most bands, including the Heartbreakers, can shake these off as problems that simply go with the territory. Such types of violence are absorbed by the mob scene but are not necessarily a product of that mob scene. In the whole of Heartbreakers history, however, there was one mob scene, in the winter of 1978, that definitely haunted Petty throughout his long career.

It was in San Francisco at the Winterland Ballroom on December 30. Petty went to the edge of the stage and the audience sunk its claws in: "It was in '78 that it dawned on me about the audience. We had only been playing big rooms a little while and we went into Winterland. I think Bruce [Springsteen] had been in there two nights before, and he built a lower stage across the front and it was still there. We weren't using it because the kids had all their jackets and everything piled up. So by the end of the night I was just getting a little bit playful and went out, jumped down, just leaned over the crowd."

Petty was pulled down into the massive surge of bodies and it took four roadies to extricate him: "I really thought I was gonna die, because there was no air. And I couldn't even see, everything went dark. . . . Like we're gonna die right here in the middle of this mob." He feared they would split him into a million tiny relics: "It was very violent in the sense that they were all going to take a finger and a leg. . . . They're crazy people when they're that worked up. I remember that night when it dawned on us: we can't go down there." Springsteen had built out this low stage precisely so he could go down there, and Petty continued to reflect on the contrast between their audiences even years later: "I've noticed that I can't get near an audience as Bruce Springsteen does. They rip me up. Bruce can walk through them. I think they look at him as their buddy. With me, there seems to be some violent or sexual vibes. I'm the last guy on earth to be violent."

Even as he distanced himself from violent inclinations, he did own the vibe in his crowd: "Ever since then I've been a little nervous about getting near the edge of the stage. I've seen these bands that dive onto the people and get passed around. Well, my crowd just tears you to bits. It's a funny thing; it still stays in my mind." The Winterland incident was over in less than two minutes, yet Petty repeatedly emphasized that the effect of it upon his stage presence lasted a lifetime: "It's like one minute you're doing a rock 'n' roll show, and the next minute you're in fear for your life. I think that's the only time that's ever happened to me. But it really did something in my head and has always stuck in the back of my mind."

Also in San Francisco, at the Fillmore in 1997, some dirtbag set off a can of pepper spray in the middle of the crowd. The paramedics were called in because dozens of ticket holders were having trouble breathing and the mob scene caused a forty-five-minute delay. This was on the second night of the Heartbreakers doing twenty shows in thirty days there, and Petty was ambivalent about it: "The second night was maybe one of my best nights . . . ever. In fact, it was going so good I kind of thought the fuse was going to blow." If he was too good, the mob made a scene. Down in Los Angeles, his three-night stint at the Forum nearly got cancelled: "I remember being shut down after the first [show]. The fire marshals were very upset at how out of control the crowd was and wanted to cancel the next two nights. We really had to do a song and dance for the fire department."

It's not just that something was up with the fans in California, or that the late seventies saw a lot of concert violence. It didn't get better in the eighties or abroad. Tench said, "When we toured [*Long After Dark*] in Europe, in the middle of 'Straight Into Darkness' for about four or five gigs in a row, fights broke out. It didn't matter if we were playing a regular gig or an army base or what, fights would break out in the middle of that song." At his home studio in 1984, Petty famously punched a wall in frustration during the *Southern Accents* sessions, pulverizing his left hand. At thirty-four, he could still be quite cantankerous with himself and with his band members. During the Dylan gigs in 1986, he reported that he and Lynch "got in a big fight, and I left the stage. Stan was wound-up about something, and he gave me the middle finger during the show. I just took my guitar and walked off. Left. They didn't know what to do."

Even when he or his band were not directly channeling the malignancies inside their own mob scene, that violence still found its way to meet them. In 1989 at the MTV Music Video Awards, Petty performed "Free Fallin'" with Guns N' Roses, and, as they walked offstage, Vince Neil of Mötley Crüe sucker punched guitarist Izzy Stradlin. When asked about it much later, Petty shrugged, "Well, you know us. We manage to get into shit somehow." That "somehow" is wide open, isn't it? Even as a cartoon in 2002, Petty got into some shit. Starring as himself among the guests assembled for rock camp in the "How I Spent My Strummer Vacation" episode of *The Simpsons*, he somehow lost a toe on his right foot after Mick Jagger drove a fire-spewing float of Satan's head into their audience in order to force Homer to stop getting wild onstage. The mob rioted and Petty never found his toe.

Mysticism

Rolling Stone's Mikal Gilmore once declared that "Petty's commitment to rock 'n' roll approaches religious fervor." Indeed, I think any commitment to rock music ought to be categorized as such. There is a certain degree of mysticism that necessarily accompanies every rock concert because that's just what happens when you get a big audience to focus their attention on what's happening on the stage. That communal experience produces a massive release of collective emotions. Phenomenologically, the Saturday night show and the Sunday morning service have just about everything in common.

Petty sensed it immediately as a kid: "When I met Elvis, we didn't really have a conversation. I was introduced by my uncle, and he sort of grunted my way. What stays with me is the whole scene. I had never seen a real mob scene before. I was really young and impressionable. Elvis really did look—he looked sort of not real, as if he were glowing. He was astounding, even spiritual. It was like a procession in church: a line of white Cadillacs and mohair suits and pompadours so black, they were blue."

Rock stars are not simply preachers; they are gods. Petty recalled, "Elvis appeared like a vision. Elvis didn't look like the people I'd known. He had a real glow about him, like a full-body halo. He looked like a god to me. After I saw Elvis that one time, I became obsessed. I can't tell you how much rock 'n' roll consumed me. It wasn't a matter of choice. It was something that came over me like a disease. I went home a changed man."

From the beginning, his audiences latched on to that disease. After the Heartbreakers' first gigs opening for Blondie at the Whisky a Go Go in 1977, Gilmore said, "It's all powerful testimony, and the audience fans the spirit with a volley of exhortations and clenched fists." Petty said, "You go to these shows, and they're *so* frantic. I don't know if everyone realizes it, but these shows, they're downright *frenzied*. It's so loud that sometimes you can't really do quiet songs. It's so *loud*. The audience is so loud sometimes that they can almost drown us out." The music industry went into similar frenzy over the band's instigation of major litigation hassles. As early as 1981, Campbell was ready to declare, "Maybe the reason it's taken us so long to succeed is that Tom pisses people off. For as long as I've known him he's bugged people in authority."

It sure looked like a good deal when observing Elvis from the outside, but once Petty achieved star status for himself, he saw how ugly it could get. In addition to powering through concert mayhem like at Winterland and a string of legal battles, Petty felt increasingly infringed upon in his personal life. In 1980, the day after his thirtieth birthday, Petty's mother died. He was forced to stay home because "he worried that he'd turn his own mother's funeral into a mob scene." In 1987, he had his own brush with death at the hands of some crazed idiot who set Petty's house on fire. They were supposed to be celebrating his wife's birthday with a party that evening but woke up instead to flames and an immediate need to evacuate.

Perhaps we can forgive a concert crowd that spills over the edge into frenzy from time to time. Petty formed a band and stepped onto the stage somewhat courting but at a minimum accepting the attendant possible risks. It's another matter entirely to receive a surprise arson in your own home. He never really learned who did it or why: "I spent a lot of time trying to figure it out, but I realized I couldn't. That's the hardest thing, realizing that somebody did it. . . . Damn, I don't know, I don't dwell on it much—I did wonder about who did it, but I will never know. The impulse is to use reason to understand something that lives beyond reason."

Beyond reason lies radical uncertainty, which the arson incident required Petty to confront once again: "It's one of those crazy things that happens to you and makes you aware there's a lot of unbalanced activity out there, and you don't see it until it has happened. How can you not feel vulnerable? But the choice is to hang in fear, looking over your shoulder, or to start counting your blessings. It's not much of a choice, really." The mob scene makes us feel vulnerable, but Petty pushed on, "When my mind drifts toward the negative, the how-could-this-happen line of thinking, I pull that image up [of Annie Lennox buying a new wardrobe for the Petty family]. It's more lasting. It's more crucial." His daughter Adria's assessment of the situation was similar. The incident reminded her that "we're all we've got, and that was cool."

Real love was their salvation, and the fire cemented in Petty a sense that he could no longer take his foundations for granted: "[The arson] was so vicious and angry that it completely scared all of that out of me. I didn't want to do anything except sing really light, happy music after that. In retrospect, I wanted to go to some much lighter place. I was really glad to be alive. I was like someone who had survived a plane crash. You are just really glad that they didn't get you. If you've ever had anybody try to kill you, it really makes you re-evaluate everything. I came away with the realization that stuff is temporary."

The violence of Petty's career had left its mark on him:

> I was pretty turbulent, looking back at it. I was a pretty turbulent person. I don't think I was an asshole. But I think I was intense. *Very* intense. So I don't think it was always somebody else's fault. I'll take the blame as much as anyone else [*laughs*] for what went on. But I was very intense, very serious about this. We were going to do it. We were going to make something *great*. And sometimes that requires a lot of intensity. I think it was just born into me. I'm *incredibly* changed. I think I'm a much-changed person from those days. I think I'm a lot mellower.

Out of necessity, this mellowing proliferated into all-important facets of Petty's existence: "I had taken intensity about as far as it could go in my personal life and with the guys in the band and business people and everybody. I realized I couldn't go on living so intense and revved up and stuff. Because, with some kind of flash realization, I realized that I had actually never really enjoyed myself. I'd done partying and I'd done work but I'd never genuinely enjoyed myself." Fulfillment was on the way in the form of touring as Bob Dylan's backing band, an enormous wellspring of education and inspiration from which all the Heartbreakers drew.

When they were joined by the Grateful Dead on that 1986 tour, Petty particularly noted a difference between his own audiences and theirs: "I gotta say, when we did that first show I looked out at the crowd and I still haven't gotten over it. Those Deadheads gave me a whole new respect for that band . . . I had no idea. I mean, it's easy to laugh at, but that audience is a whole social phenomenon. It's like the '60s in a way, but I found it very healthy. Those people were so charged up, they listened—really listened—to every little lick we played from the first note of the show." Where the Heartbreakers' crowd drowned the band out, the Dead's crowd listened to the band acutely. Where his fans were frenzied, theirs were simply charged at a healthy level. Petty covered the Dead's "Friend of the Devil" for his San Francisco residency at the Fillmore in 1997 and revived it again for the Beacon and Fonda residencies in 2013.

Petty is no straightforward kind of hippie. You could transplant the redneck to California, but how much redneck could you really take out of the man? He'd previously found the peaceable vibe of the Deadheads laughable but ultimately came to envy their far more mellow version of a concert crowd. Petty had mistakenly believed that rock 'n' roll shows channeled the audience's darkness, that this was the only way to induce a proper release in a mob scene and that the mob scene was inherently rooted in some collective darkness. On tour with Dylan and the Grateful Dead, he came to understand that it was possible to gather an audience to himself by channeling their light instead of their darkness, and a mob scene predicated on that was no less mystical. He'd been skinning some of the lives off his cat the hard way.

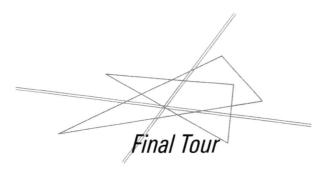

Final Tour

Atlanta Show

Tom Petty and the Heartbreakers turned forty in 2017, celebrating with a summer arena tour. The Phillips Arena show was their fifth gig and showcased the same set list as the previous three gigs, despite Petty's comments during the planning stages that gave consideration to the possibility of more flexible set lists and some obscure cuts. The concert proved that this was a band with a deep bench of singles, and, over the course of nineteen songs, the band touched on nearly every album in its extensive catalog.

The one rarity of the bunch was the very first song of the night, "Rockin' Around (With You)," the first track on the band's self-titled debut album from 1976. TPHB hadn't played it since the early eighties, but there was no more fitting way to begin to reflect on their four decades of "one-hundred percent rock and roll," as Petty shouted when he took the stage wearing a purple jacket and vest. The Heartbreakers were sporting a variety of cool hats on their shaggy heads, with pianist Benmont Tench in a Panama, lead guitarist Mike Campbell in a deadman's topper, and versatile sideman Scott Thurston in a porkpie.

The gang also welcomed two new backup singers, the Webb Sisters. Since 2008, English sibling duo Charley and Hattie had the pleasure of working with dearly departed Leonard Cohen when he reemerged to tour again after a fifteen-year hiatus. Petty saw them play with Cohen and said, "It's been a dream of mine" to work with them and that taking them on the tour "really makes the boys behave." Their harp and guitar skills were not in evidence that night, but they did occasionally play tambourine in addition to contributing backing vocals for the entire set. Sometimes Petty himself accompanied them as backup while turning the main vocals over to the crowd, as on "Learning to Fly" and "I Won't Back Down," when he encouraged the audience by commenting, "You know, I can hear you singin' all the way up here, and it's a lovely sound." There was also early speculation that opener Joe Walsh might sit in for a song or two, but the band remained focused on what they had always delivered as an island unto themselves.

Petty told the crowd that he wanted to "just touch down all the way through those forty years." As on their previous tours, there was little consideration for fancy special effects or eye-catching background videos. They ran old photographs of the band and included clips from their storied run of artistic videography from the early days of MTV. Many of those clips are as iconic as the songs in them, such as "Don't Come Around Here No More," which was perhaps the only somewhat melancholy song of the evening. At least once per decade, Petty writes an album that really digs into his down-tempo and sneering cynicism, as in 1987's *Let Me Up (I've Had Enough)*, 1999's *Echo*, and 2002's *The Last DJ*. But the albums where Petty had a serious bone to pick are not often indulged in concert, and they are not really represented in the final tour's greatest hits set list.

One of the band's most unusual works was the soundtrack for 1996's romantic comedy *She's the One*, critically praised but seldom heard in concert. Petty noted, "This is a song we hardly ever get to play, but I wanted to play it," and then the band broke out "Walls." Their bandleader did not tend to be chatty during shows, and he generally kept things light when he did banter. Petty didn't wade into presidential politics in part because he knew a lot of his fans, especially in the South, might disagree with him. Instead, he just stood at the mic, smiling over the new implication toward Donald Trump's insistence on building a bigger Mexican border wall as he sang "even walls fall down." During "Forgotten Man," they rolled footage of homeless people sleeping in front of the White House. The band didn't like to make a big deal about it, but they did get cheeky with references sometimes upon close examination. At the first show on the tour, they rolled out "American Dream Plan B," but it got nixed for subsequent shows.

Many of the tracks from *She's the One* actually began as options for 1994's *Wildflowers*, which is technically billed as a solo album despite the fact that all the Heartbreakers other than original drummer Stan Lynch played on it. Petty had been talking a lot about his interest in doing a reissue that same year for the complete *Wallflowers* double album that he originally intended to make, and then also doing a tour of smaller venues to strip things down and really consider how that album hangs together. Those plans were put on a back burner for the big anniversary tour, but it was evident that the band was gearing up to head in that direction soon.

The Atlanta set list showcased five out of the fifteen *Wildflowers* songs. *Full Moon Fever*, Petty's 1989 solo album of twelve tracks, also featured heavily with four out of its five singles. To do the math, nine of the night's nineteen songs were from albums where the Heartbreakers did not have their name on the cover. Despite Petty's predictable pendulum swings toward these mildly more isolationist phases of creativity, it was clear that the band still felt as much ownership over the songs wrought in those moments as over the ones where they got proper billing. After all, some of these men have known each other since they were knee-high to a grasshopper. The secret of their success was a willingness to let bygones be bygones and focus on the good vibes of their music. When introducing Tench, Petty chuckled, "We've known each other since eleven years old. His mother didn't want me around, 'cause I was a bad influence."

After forty years, the mutual good influence between them was a given. Petty still delivered that nasal twang without mimicking his own studio vocals too closely or becoming a caricature of himself. Campbell could meander through waves of sustains as clear as a bell, and he was showing off a resurgent commitment to playing with slides and his whammy bar to muddy things up. Steve Ferrone continued to make it look easy, swinging away at his drum kit without ever breaking a sweat. Scott Thurston remained the member with the sharpest instinct for filling in the glue wherever it was needed. Tench contributed an ethereal gloss to everything he touched, floating honky-tonk fills that never jumped at the low-hanging fruit of the obvious notes.

They were still tight, and they knew what they could do best. Early in the show, Petty reminded the audience, "We still make new records, and we try really hard on 'em." There were two ways of looking at a band as predictable as Tom Petty and the Heartbreakers: some would dismiss them as a stale legacy act, but others could see a distillation of their essence. I was in the latter camp. As a serious Pettyhead who waited for B-sides in concert with bated breath, even I had to admit that TPHB's approach was what an anniversary tour should look like.

Of about fifty shows this summer, the band was booked in four places where they were doing two nights of shows back-to-back. No doubt there were many fans who had tickets to both shows in Milwaukee or Boston or New York. The first of these four two-night stands was in Colorado, at Red Rocks. I had never been to Red Rocks, and I had tickets to both nights. Surely the band would need to take a different approach on the second night. Wondered what it would be. They really did have enough singles that had been left off the current set list to make a second list based off of nothing but the hits. But this would be fifteen dates into the tour rather than five, and the band might want to amuse itself with some B-sides by then. "Straight Into Darkness" was a good choice to replace the current *Long After Dark* track in the list, "You Got Lucky." The lyrics themselves reflected the band's early feelings on their first tour of England, and for those just loosely hanging on to the refrain, the journey from that darkness to "Don't Come Around Here No More," the next song on the set list, was also a smooth fit.

Set Lists 1

When the fortieth-anniversary tour rolled through Houston two nights later, Petty subbed in "Crawling Back to You" for "Time to Move On." At the New Orleans Jazz and Heritage Festival, he busted out "Swingin'» for the first time since 1999, in the third slot of the night after "Last Dance with Mary Jane." He stuck "Good Enough" in where "Walls" was, so I guess one rarity is quite enough for a festival set. "Crawling Back to You" stuck around, and he eliminated "You Wreck Me" from the encore, which I suppose is the polite thing to do when you're sharing a stage with so many other bands.

"Good Enough" stuck around for the Austin set, where Gary Clark Jr. guested on it, and then "Walls" returned for the first Florida date. The set list subsequently remained unchanged for over a week, until they covered Chuck Berry's "Carol" in place of "You Wreck Me" during the encore in St. Louis, the most appropriate place for it, since Berry had settled there and recently died. "You Wreck Me" returned the following night. There was a two-week break until the Red Rocks shows.

The first time Tom Petty and the Heartbreakers played back-to-back shows at Red Rocks was in 1986, where they served as Bob Dylan's backing band. Dylan would have been in charge of the set lists, but what did Petty learn from that? Of the twenty-four songs they played each night, Dylan swapped out just four of them and made zero changes in sequencing. The changes were made in slots two, six, eight, and twenty-three—enough at the opening for those who attended the previous night to be gratified that changes were made, and a nice surprise in the encore. Twenty of the songs remained the same. That's 83 percent of the same music. If you're buying two nights at Red Rocks, I suppose it's in part because you've got the music on repeat at home anyway. So, does it matter if the second set is much the same as the first?

Fifteen years later, in 2001, Tom Petty and the Heartbreakers got their own back-to-back nights at Red Rocks. There were nineteen songs in the first set, and eighteen in the second. They cut one Merle Haggard cover. They swapped out two songs: in slot nine, a Booker T. and the M.G.'s cover became a cover of the Ventures, and in slot thirteen, "Into the Great Wide Open" became "Refugee." They also changed the sequence of two songs: "Mary Jane's Last Dance" switched with "Too Much Ain't Enough" from slot fifteen to slot five, and "Learning to Fly" moved from slot fourteen to slot twelve. That's a slightly higher percentage of the same music than Dylan's two sets contained.

The Heartbreakers did back-to-back nights there again the next year, in 2002, three nights in 2005, two nights in 2010, and three again in 2014. They did like to play at Red Rocks, which is bound to make the jams longer. In 2002 they made two song swaps, two sequencing changes, and eliminated "Too Much Ain't Enough" as well as added a cover of the Plastic Ono Band's "Give Peace a Chance." This was coming up on the one-year anniversary of the September 11 terrorist attacks. In 2005, between the first and second nights, there were two swaps and one sequencing change; on the third night there were two swaps from the first night. In 2010 they made two swaps, two sequencing changes, and two additions where eliminations might usually be. They added a cover of Fleetwood Mac's "Oh Well," plus, ironically, "Takin' My Time." One of the swaps was a cover of Them's "Mystic Eyes" for their own "American Girl" in the encore. Is 2010's June 1 show possibly the only time in their lives that they did not play "American Girl" at a concert? In 2014, between the first and second nights there was one swap and two additional covers featuring a guest appearance by Steve Winwood. On the third night there was once again a swap in the fourth song slot and a cover swap in the slot that previously included Winwood. At best, the evolution of their set list can be characterized as examples of light tinkering, with an occasional nod to the specific time, place, or special guest.

Given that this was their fortieth-anniversary tour, which Petty kept saying might be their last big one, and the fact that Red Rocks is a favorite or bucket list venue for many musicians, it was hard to understand why there hadn't been a rotating cast of all-stars. The opener was Joe Walsh, and even he hadn't stepped onstage during the main event. The band continued to be rock steady and going it alone. Perhaps they were cranky about any public pressure to deviate or dress things up, digging in their heels after having acquiesced to playing "American Girl" for all eternity.

In conclusion, the chance of my getting to hear "Straight into Darkness" during either night at Red Rocks stood technically at nonzero but, realistically, given all available evidence, I mean, c'mon. They've played it about thirty times in concert. Sixteen of those were while touring the *Long After Dark* album. It's more rare than the famously rare "Swingin'" or "Girl on LSD." They hadn't played it in almost ten years, since 2008, and they had never played it at Red Rocks. It was not going to happen.

Red Rocks Show 1

On a map, Red Rocks looks like a navigational nightmare. When you actually go there and see it, it bears no resemblance to the map. There's a lot of waiting: in the car as the line slowly wends its way toward the box office entrance, in the line for tickets that stretches out over a mile of blacktop sloping further up the ridge, in the car again to one of five parking lots, and across a mile of stairs in front of a security gate. Red Rocks presents many obstacles to the huge audiovisual payoff it promises, and it is hard to determine a strategy no matter how many times you've been there. The lady in line behind us at the gate repeatedly worried she should've gone down to get up, rather than going up to get down, as we did. And she was from Denver. But the trials began much earlier.

The box office opened four hours before the show began. Mindy and I got separated. She parked the rental minivan while I stood in the line for the tickets with my name on them. Red Rocks holds just under ten thousand people, and maybe two thousand of them were in the box office line in front of me. After fifteen minutes and no visible movement, a staffer materialized, walking down the line and asking if anybody had a last name beginning with S through Z. That's me. She said, "Go to the front. There's no line at your window." I stepped out and vaulted over a thousand people. As I ascended to the plaintive groans of folks with last names like Johnson or Carter, the staffer said, "I guess Tom Petty loves people with weird last names." I paused to reflect on the names of other people who have most extensively studied Tom Petty—Zanes, Zollo.

After handing over my identification, I was given a small stapled packet of cards. The front one had my name and billing address on it. Then there were two tickets and a receipt—and then three more cards. Those three, stapled to mine, belonged to one Kelly Voorhees of Austin, Texas. Kelly's seats were in the fourth row and mine were in the fifty-third. Mindy had dumped the van in the first available spot on the side of the road like everyone was doing and hiked back to find me puzzling over the ticketing error. Should we return Kelly's tickets to the box office? Should we use Kelly's tickets ourselves? Should we scalp them? Scalp ours and use Kelly's? The seats were so good. I blew an entire paycheck to be here.

We returned the tickets to the box office. The lady in the window verified the error immediately. It seemed Kelly had been in front of me in the line somewhere. They had printed new tickets when this set was discovered missing. The lady turned to the other staffers in the box office and said, "Mystery revealed, people! This kind, honest woman just returned the Voorhees pack that was lost. The packs were stapled together. Be careful what you're doing!" We'd passed the first test. The Red Rocks box office dubbed us kind and honest women.

Next we would choose a parking lot. Three traffic cops directed us to three possible options. We chose the highest road and would pass through a cave to reach the Upper North. Rains came down, and tailgaters took shelter on their bumpers, beneath their open Subaru trunks. We inched forward on the stairs, braving an ogre carrying a plastic cup full of Crown Royal. Sean, the lone possessor of an earpiece who also had a windbreaker with "Supervisor" embroidered on it, assured me this line was the right one to get to our dinner. He had my name on a list that never left his left hand. Later, when the line stopped moving, he walked down asking for anybody with dinner reservations at Ship Rock Grille. Once again, we vaulted over a thousand people. Sean said, "I never walk the line this far, but I knew you were back there somewhere." He winked and said he'd look out for us tomorrow too.

There were two nice T-shirts, so I hemmed and hawed a little. Turned out that the one I settled on was available only in small and extra large, so I got the other one. It came with a Red Rocks seventy-fifth-anniversary banner. In a sea of ten thousand people, we went to a restroom and ran into two ladies from Phoenix who'd randomly been in the same shop as us in downtown Denver three days before. One of them hugged us. I got Mindy a hoodie for a third layer, but we would freeze our balls off anyway. First we went to our buffet, where we were greeted by Logan of the pink-and-blue hairdo. She loved Mindy's outfit and gave us the best seats in the restaurant. Said she'd look out for us tomorrow too. A heap of pork loin, orecchiette, snap peas, and cheesecake later, we could hear instrumental tinkering that meant Joe Walsh was getting ready to take the stage.

We waited out the last of the drizzle by walking through the Red Rocks Hall of Fame. There was some autographed stuff, a wall collaged with beautiful old concert posters, a giant documentary video screen, and three walls of portraits featuring those musicians who'd played the most legendary shows there. Each plaque listed relevant details such as the number of shows a musician had played or a quote about Red Rocks. Petty's plaque said he fought to keep record prices low. It included a photo with the olive-green velour jacket and a red scarf. Bono's plaque talked about the U2 concert video that launched a million pilgrimages to Red Rocks.

Then, from the top side, we went into the amphitheater. Walsh primed the audience to chime in with a grunt and fist pump during a particular chorus by practicing it with us before the song started. He said,

"I know it seems silly, but just do it. Trust me. Tonight when you're goin' down the mountain, you'll think to yourself, 'I made a huge difference today.'" The sardonic tone made the best argument for including him as the opener. We laughed, and then, when the big moment came, everyone indeed grunted. The previous bout of sarcasm made it better, added that dose of ironic, transcendent distance.

Petty's set list was exactly as anticipated. What caught me off guard was the extent to which his banter and gestures were also repeats of the Atlanta show. He began with "We're gonna play one hundred percent rock and roll music for you tonight." He made the joke about how "Walls" was being played at his own request. He did conducting big arms, crucifixion big arms, airplane big arms, and bowing big arms, as usual. But he also rested his forehead on the mic for the same long moment of a particular song, such that I began to wonder if touching mic to brain was one of those prayerful things he was evolving into a way to punctuate the big arms repertoire or if he workshopped it in over the course of this show as a more specialized effect. Either way, it became clear to me that the total effect of these repetitions was neither boring nor disappointing. In fact, I could geek out on the subtleties of variations. From my seats on the floor at the Atlanta show, the lighted orbs hanging over the stage seemed lame. From the fifty-third row at Red Rocks, looking down on the orbs, I could see they were making all kinds of snakes and shapes, and the visual was cool.

Regardless of the sameness or difference, or same-same-but-differentness, of these performances, I found myself searching for "Straight into Darkness." When we sat down, Mindy had asked me what song I was most excited to hear. Without thinking, I said, "The song that he'll never play." Of course, I meant the song that is the subject of these essays, but the wider, more bittersweet implications made me chuckle. Throughout the night, I occasionally hoped against hope, when Petty said, "We haven't played this song in twenty years" or "This one is by special request." But moreover, I found all the elements of "Straight into Darkness" present in other ways. I cried during "Free Fallin'," was grateful for my wife during "Wreck Me," examined the shifting meanings of repeating lines during "You Got Lucky," basked in the uncertainty of "American Girl," steeled myself with "I Won't Back Down," dove into the surrealism of "Don't Come Around Here No More," even settled into the contentment of "Wildflowers." "You Got Lucky" is somebody else's rarity, right off the same album as mine, achingly close.

All the parts of my love for "Straight into Darkness" were revealed elsewhere, in disparate pieces that I would cobble together inside the crystal clear sonic majesty of Red Rocks. I brought my earplugs and never used them—not a bit of ringing when we left the parking lot, which we accomplished with surprising speed and ease under a starry sky with its slivered moon hanging low in the windshield. The mountains were invisible in the pitch-black night. We'd taken the same road out that we took in, and everything about it was different in the darkness. Tomorrow, we'd do it again.

Red Rocks Show 2

And on the second day, we did it again. There was no wait at the box office. The ticket pack was correct. We took a side trail to the Colorado Music Hall of Fame, which largely consisted of a room full of John Denver artifacts and a gift shop. They didn't have the T-shirt I wanted yesterday. The tour buses were parked nearby in a dirt lot. We could hear the sound check as we returned to the minivan.

I distinctly heard the opening bars of "Swingin'." Maybe the boys were just noodling, but the obvious implication was that they might play it that night. They'd played it at Jazz Fest earlier. No matter how often the set list seems like a closed case, predestined and set in stone, I always find a way to notice the nonzero chance of changes.

We parked in a different spot in the same lot and lounged around, our waiting marked by various Tom Petty B-sides and rarities drifting out the back of neighboring cars. Nobody played "Straight into Darkness." It was seventy-three degrees and the sun was shining. I'd already gotten burnt while sitting outside our cabin recording my impressions of last night. A big, friendly Saint Bernard with curly hair kept wading into Bear Creek and then loping over to say hello without shaking off on me. The dog reminded me of Joe Walsh, and I'd started humming "Life's Been Good to Me So Far."

On this pilgrimage, I'd steeled myself for the wrong type of violence. In our short wait at the security gate, there were some friendly gentlemen drinking beers in line behind us. One of them had just landed from a delayed flight, left his bags in the car, and rushed right over to Red Rocks so as not to miss anything. He'd seen the band several times before, but this was a bucket list venue for him. He was just like us—until he wilted midsentence, his eyes rolling back as a seizure sent him skull-first down onto the concrete with a hard thud somewhat dulled by his baseball cap. As he convulsed on the ground, the cap came off his bald head and we could see the blood pooling in it. It was a wide cut, but not spurting.

He was already safely on his side. I yelled for a medic and for the crowd to part but forgot to start counting. He'd been down about ten seconds when I finally got the attention of the yellow-jacketed parking lot manager. She radioed for the ambulance ready nearby, cleared the cars, and then cleared the humans. Some assholes were worried about losing their places in line. One particular major bastard commented that the guy on the ground spent four hundred bucks for nothing. His wife hissed at him to shut up. The medics arrived within ninety seconds and the guy had stopped bleeding. His breathing was labored but his eyes were focused.

They took my statement and carted off the guy, who'd been in line alone. Mindy and the lady in line directly behind us turned around so as not to stare at the puddle of blood that remained on the ground. The puddle was gone when we walked back that way to leave after the show. Poor guy. Hopefully they gave him a fresh ticket. Never got his name, but I suppose we'll remember him forever. Was a little salty with myself for forgetting to count how long he had seized; I'm good in a crisis, but nobody's perfect. When the unforeseen strikes, you just have to roll with it.

On that second night, Walsh made the same joke, and it still worked. Petty came on talking about "a hunnet puh-cent" rock and roll, and it still worked. He wore the brown fringe jacket, and Campbell wore the purple velvet one. I've always thought it was cute and brotherly how they shared crazy jackets, and wondered which one feels the shoulders are a bit tight and which one thinks the sleeves are too long. Midway through the same set list as the previous night, the lightning arrived. We fiercely booed the announcement of a ten-minute break, to which Petty responded, "We don't like it any more than you do."

Red Rocks has a curfew set by the local noise ordinance. You can go till 11 or maybe 11:15. This storm delay cut into the band's best-laid plans. We herded toward the sides of the venue to get a little bit of shelter from the walls while the crew scurried around throwing tarps over everything on the stage. There was a brief downpour, and the concession stands delayed their last call. Like a dumbass, I accidentally left my backpack under the seat, and Mindy and I were separated so she could stay dry while I retrieved it.

The band came back on twenty-two minutes later. Even playing long pushed up against the curfew; wouldn't they still need to cut something? Would they swap in a rarity to reward the fans for staying? Petty had changed into the green army jacket, and claimed that the crew, unused to a break in the middle of the set, had taken advantage of the extra time by getting drunk. He came on muttering in a singsong granny voice that was still half-serious, "Better safe than saaaah-reeee." I was thinking about that afternoon sound check and holding my breath for "Swingin'." They played it, and it was good.

Seemed like they'd cut something from the *Wildflowers* portion of the set to accommodate "Swingin'," but Petty is a true redneck—unwilling to be told what to do by either weather or lawful curfew. He cut nothing from his planned selection of tunes. Moreover, due to a monitor failure brought on by the rain and a board failure brought on by the crew's drunkenness, Petty couldn't hear his acoustic for a solo. During the wait, Tench began noodling around on some rockabilly, Campbell picked it up, they brought Petty another electric, and the band launched into Chuck Berry's "Carol." Two songs got added and none were swapped or eliminated, for a tour record of twenty-one songs. These changes accommodated the audience based on genuine surprise fails of weather and technology. No quarter was given to the local noise ordinance, for the church of rock and roll is higher than the laws of this land.

Set Lists 2

Marty Stuart was a guest on "Crawling Back to You" at the New York festival gig on June 17. On June 24 at the Rose Bowl, "Into the Great Wide Open" was subbed in for "Walls," and the band continued to sub it in on June 29 in Chicago, then Philly. "Walls" returned to its slot after these three shows.

The next back-to-back shows were at Milwaukee Summerfest. For the first show, "Into the Great Wide Open" replaced "You Got Lucky," with "Walls" holding steady in its original spot. "You Got Lucky" returned for the second show, knocking out "Into the Great Wide Open." At London's Hyde Park on July 9, special guest Stevie Nicks meant "Stop Draggin' My Heart Around" was inserted before the Wildflowers set. "You Got Lucky" was booted to make time for it, and it stayed gone for the next three gigs until the band got to Boston, even though "Stop Draggin' My Heart Around" disappeared when Nicks did.

Boston was a two-night stand. On the first night, "You Got Lucky" returned to its usual spot. On the second night, it was replaced by "Into the Great Wide Open" while "Walls" was replaced by "Swingin'." In Baltimore the next night, "Swingin'" got to stay. Then there were back-to-back shows in Forest Hills, New York, home of the Ramones. The first night's set was the same as Baltimore's, except "Wreck Me" was cut from the encore. The second night employed the set list from the first of their two nights in Milwaukee. It replaced "You Got Lucky" with "Into the Great Wide Open" and "Swingin'" with "Walls."

Where did "Wreck Me" go? It returned to the encore in Philly, where the set list was otherwise the same as the second night in New York. Then the band went on break for two weeks before the final leg of the tour, which included two three-night stands at the Greek and the Hollywood Bowl. At the time of the break, the set lists had so far possessed a striking amount of rigidity even when the band performed two nights in the same place. The only example of genuine deviation was the Chuck Berry detour on the second night at Red Rocks, after Petty's guitar got too wet and Tench bought the crew a few extra minutes with his improvisational boogie.

After the two-week break, the set list from Philly traveled to Vancouver and then Seattle. The band then headed back to California for the final leg of the tour. They'd scheduled the three shows at the Greek in Berkeley for August 22, 23, and 27. The latter two shows ended up on August 28 and 30, having been rescheduled because Petty had met his old nemesis, laryngitis. The fans didn't know at the time, but Petty had also done the entire tour with a hairline fracture in his left hip, causing him a great deal of pain each night, so the postponement served more purpose than just that stated one. The August 25 Sacramento show also got rescheduled for September 1.

Those three shows at the Greek mirrored the Heartbreakers' very first tour, when they'd done three sold-out shows at the Keystone, less than a mile away. That was when "American Girl" was a brand new tune at the top of the set list rather than the ultimate closer, and when they could sell out the Keystone in Berkeley but then face just twenty people the next night at the other Keystone in Palo Alto.

The first two nights at the Greek were identical to the rest of the fortieth-anniversary tour. On the third night, "Into the Great Wide Open" was switched out for "Breakdown," which had also been a top hit in 1977 and hadn't been in the touring rotation since 2010. "Breakdown" poses an odd lyrical perpendicularity when followed by the usual next bit on the set list, "I Won't Back Down."

"Breakdown" hung around for the Sacramento show, and after a two-week break, that song slot was entirely cut out for the festival head-lining gig in San Diego. Finally, in late September, after fifty shows in twenty-four states, Tom Petty and the Heartbreakers returned home to close their fortieth-anniversary tour with three nights at the Hollywood Bowl. The slot that held "Into the Great Wide Open" and "Breakdown" remained cut on the first night, but "Into the Great Wide Open" re-turned on the second night after a shake-up that moved "I Won't Back Down" and "Free Fallin'" ahead of it. "Walls" was eliminated instead.

The last show once again replaced "Into the Great Wide Open" with "Breakdown." Throughout the tour, the *Wildflowers* section of the set list was never touched, nor was "American Girl" ever moved from its en-core-closing slot. The Heartbreakers had played "American Girl" more than seven hundred times in concert since 1977.

The main move to chart across set lists from this tour was the coming and going of "Into the Great Wide Open," which had been seen in concert about one hundred and fifty times since its debut in 1991, a couple more times than "Walls" since its debut in 1996. "Into the Great Wide Open" is about the perils of rock stardom, of going to Hollywood. The great wide open symbolizes both the glory of limitless possibility and the terror of not having a clue as to how to proceed.

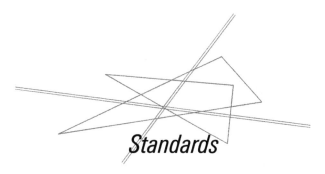

Standards

Individualism

Tom Petty had always been his own toughest critic: "I'm pretty rough on myself, as far as giving a pat on the back." As bandleader of the Heartbreakers, he assumed the obligation of shepherding their career in a manner that cultivated longevity. At a minimum, this meant he set the goals of the band: "I know what the objective is, what we've gotta pull off, which is a lot of the game." But the cost of this was that "everyone tells me I'm a control freak. Maybe I am. Because I notice all the details. That was a characteristic I developed from having this huge responsibility on my back."

Maintaining a successful trajectory was not simply a matter of cranking out one album after another. The devil is in the details because each album had to build on what came before it. Petty said, "You can accomplish a goal, but it doesn't mean anything if you don't accomplish it right." He drilled down obsessively into the particulars because that was how he could continue to do something new with each successive product. Said Warren Zanes, "Petty was a student of the Beatles, which meant he believed that every album needed to be different from the last. They didn't make Rubber Soul twice."

Petty confirmed, "You know, before The Beatles, you didn't really see rock stars trying to evolve. They were *quite* happy to have a hit, and often

the follow-up was almost exactly the same." The newness Petty demanded of each album couldn't spring from the merely trendy sensibilities of
pop crap. Petty's devotion to ensuring the Heartbreakers evolved as a
band led him to police their authenticity: "I sort of like the idea—even
to this day—of refining our craft. We're trying to take what we do and
refine it, and get it a little more pure with each release. But I'm looking
for *purity*. I'm a *purist*. [*Laughs*] ... There's a thing about music: if you believe the singer, then the song is going to work. It's all about believability.
If you can believe the singer, it will work. So I think our quest was for
purity."

In the early eighties, as the band found fame, Petty balked against
admitting either that he was a purist or that his work was important. On
the contrary, he insisted, "rock & roll is just cheap shit—nothing deeper
than that." This reflects not so much his opinion or his respect for his
audience but his resistance to attention from critics: "[The rock press]
saved my ass on that first album, and I guess I'm indebted to them. But I
still get annoyed. I find it hard to believe anybody really cares that much
about what I have to say. I mean, it's only rock & roll—just disposable
crap that won't mean much in 10 years."

Petty's frustration was in finding out that the music alone doesn't
speak for itself; he was expected to do promotional rounds that would
help speak for it. His resentment made him an ornery interview, and
interviewers knew it. "He thinks he's a lousy interview," Steve Pond said
in 1981. "He's not; he's outspoken and articulate, if inclined at times to
extricate himself with self-deprecating answers: 'They're just records;
sometimes you make the best one, sometimes you don't.' Petty keeps
on giving interviews—fewer than before—not because he wants to be a
public figure but because he has to be a rock & roller."

Looking back on his dismissal of rock music's impact on the world,
Petty confessed to Pond that he should've moderated his comments
with a better sense of humor: "I felt terrible. I felt like I'd insulted

everybody by saying that. I didn't mean it's cheap shit—what we've done means an awful lot to me. But I can't approach it that seriously. I can't sit down and say, 'Here's a classic.' I've got to say it's disposable. You move on to the next thing; you can't dwell on what you've done. But if the old ones live forever, great." He believed mightily in what he was doing and in his ability to carry on doing it, but he always viewed the promotional part as a complete drag: "It's gotten where everything has gotten so media-oriented. It's almost like when you make a record, you got to be punished for it."

Petty thought of himself as too sensitive to ride a wave of publicity. It grossed him out as fakery, in clear contrast to the believability and purity he was aiming at in the music. As the securities of his rock stardom took root, he cut back on any promotional work, other than touring, as much as he could because "my mind is so delicate that I can't take being part of that. It's just like hanging around after a show to meet people. I can't do that. I don't even do interviews on the road. So I am not the best star for promoting himself. I think that's the whole problem with our career. For someone of the stature that we are, we have never embraced the promotion machine. Maybe we should have."

Even in places where the machine had served them well, like on MTV, Petty ultimately withdrew to whatever extent it was possible. He said that as videos "got more popular, the industry grew, and it became its own industry. And the films got much more expensive to make. And the record companies, to this day, have this really shitty deal, where they make you pay for the video. . . . And now a video can easily cost a million bucks. So we've pulled out of that game. We became disenchanted with it, so we just quit doing it." Journalist Neil Strauss said, "Petty is not like other artists. When asked if he'd prefer instead to disappear from the public eye like legendary recluses Sly Stone or Captain Beefheart, he goes silent for a moment, then nods his head softly. 'Yeah,' he admits, 'I can see myself that way very easily.'"

Though the interviews could be slowed to a trickle, they would never truly cease. Petty had to do them for his band, as the leader with a responsibility to help the music succeed. Albert Camus said, "I see that man going back down with a heavy yet measured step toward the torment of which he will never know the end. That hour like a breathing-space which returns as surely as his suffering, that is the hour of consciousness. At each of those moments when he leaves the heights and gradually sinks toward the lairs of the gods, he is superior to his fate. He is stronger than his rock." It is against the muddied repetitions of publicity that Petty most often revolted, trying to inject that same believability he gave to his music.

"Often the best interviews are given by the musicians who avoid them the most, like Springsteen or Eric Clapton," concluded Strauss. "And often one of the reasons they don't like to sit down for an interview is because they are too honest and sincere in these types of interactions, unwilling to go into autopilot and parrot the same answers they've given before. This is true of Petty." Petty was wary of becoming the flat, static image projected by magazines, as opposed to the nuanced, dynamic one he built with due deliberation onstage or in the studio. Publicity was not his life's work but was the sometimes-necessary cost of that work.

He tried to let the honesty of his music seep into interviews but worried that the shallowness of interviewing would ultimately pollute the music itself: "What can you do if you sell 8 million records? You're going to get a little decadent whether you know it or not. Then each release had to top the one before, and I know that pressure's coming down the line for us, too. If you let that mentality overtake you, you end up being one of those people who is afraid to run off course. But the only people who ever really make the big score are the ones who run off the course." He was known as a control freak for trying to set his own course. Petty said, "You're always competing with yourself, even a hundred songs later." Jimmy Iovine admired that Petty didn't allow others to put him off track: "Tom's the kind of proud guy who will not bend past a certain point. But over the years I've realized that the really great ones don't have to compromise. Tom is definitely one of the great ones."

Petty was certainly a prideful man, always trusting himself and the love between members of his band more than any of the music industry pressures that had been put upon them. He said, "Well, you've got all your life to write your first album, and then you've got nine months to write the second one." Even as he sought to evolve the Heartbreakers' self-concept with each new album, he set up a frozen core of standards for how to accomplish it: "You've got to stick to a standard. It's in the back of your mind. I have to stay up to a certain standard. So even with an album, everything has got to be as good as the thing before it." Every resultant album of course had to be released into their wild audience and unleashed through that disgusting promotional machine.

But these core standards for the musicianship itself imitated a constancy of creation that Petty picked up from his heroes. He said, "For so much of my life, I took rock & roll seriously. I wonder if people understand how much that meant. It was a renaissance period. Artists were doing their great work. But you took it for granted that it was just going to go on and on. It was sad to see rock & roll shoot itself in the foot. . . . It's all about greed. When people realized there were fortunes to be made with this stuff, it changed." Just as with Petty's idols, the constant quality of the Heartbreakers' work had also to some extent been the band's hobgoblin. Petty said, "As successful as [the Heartbreakers] have been, part of me thinks we have been taken for granted to a degree. Maybe that's because we have always been consistent. . . . I think maybe if we were gone, God forbid, there would be a different take on us."

For the Heartbreakers, the consistency of the music was due largely to the constancy of Petty himself. Said Benmont Tench, "Tom's not much different from the guy I first met. I was over at his house a few weeks ago, sitting around the kitchen table, and it felt pretty much the same as sitting around the kitchen table in their old apartment in Gainesville. Of course, it's a much bigger kitchen." Greed pissed them off and fame made them laugh. Humor and anger were always the band's twin coping mechanisms for all that the rock and roll life had to offer. Those were tools they couldn't quite muster in working on *Long After Dark*.

According to Zanes, Petty "says he doesn't like *Long After Dark*. But what he doesn't like is the world he was living in during that period of time. The songs tell the story of that place, more directly than the material on any previous recording. Hopelessness, loss, lust, the impossibility of love . . . without a lot of symbolism to hide behind." Zanes quoted verse one, lines three and four of "Straight Into Darkness," connecting to the dissolution of Petty's marriage to Jane. When things were going poorly at home, they were also often going poorly at work with the band. Said Petty, "Well, I'm stubborn. God knows, neither relationship has been particularly smooth. They each had real separations and frustrations along the way. I guess there is some weird parallel."

While *Long After Dark* went gold, idled on the charts, and garnered some obligatory but lackluster accolades from critics, Petty clung instead to a handful of compliments from his peers: "I've had nice moments throughout my career when an artist I admire weighs in on my material. I remember Bruce Springsteen saying something about the song 'Straight Into Darkness,' and at a time when I felt like that album, *Long After Dark*, was kind of lost on people. That meant a lot." Petty's twin efforts of personal constancy and musical evolution, considered simultaneously, yield a sense of mysticism. Jackson Browne said, "He's very mysterious. Doesn't encourage a lot of investigation into his personal circumstances. But because the songs affect us the way they do, because of the intimacy that happens in them, you're looking for a trace . . . maybe that's what he finds unnerving, the recognition that people are peering straight into him, wanting something."

In the results of 1982's *Long After Dark*, Petty felt there was nothing to see except the pressures of the industry. He was becoming an empty vessel: "I didn't even want to make that album. I liked a lot of the songs, but we seemed to be going for the same sound. I was worried that we were beginning to pander to the audience for the first time. I can see now that some of the passion was gone, and I don't think we really got it back until we went on the road with Bob." Tom Petty and the Heartbreakers served as Bob Dylan's backing band for the True Confessions Tour, from February through August 1986. Over more than fifty shows, Petty would study the wellspring of Dylan's mojo as they shared a stage, emerging with a lesson in self-preservation that would serve him well for the rest of his life. Said Zanes, "No one interferes with the mystery around Dylan, which may be his greatest creation."

Transcendence

It was while producing Del Shannon's *Drop Down and Get Me* in 1981 that Petty first began to work with his own few heroes: "There just weren't that many of my peers that got my attention like the guys I grew up listening to. If one of those artists still had the goods, I was fascinated at the idea of working with them and bringing whatever I had to the table, seeing what happened. And it went both ways, it seems. It's happened a number of times, like some of these guys were thinking, 'I want to find this kid—let's look him up.'" Petty's work with Shannon was a bright spot in the early eighties, but in 1985, he accepted an invitation from Bob Dylan. Petty said of their collaboration, "Good things seem to follow bad. It's always been that way, for me, anyway."

Dylan had previously enlisted several Heartbreakers for studio sessions. Both the band and Dylan were scheduled to play at the inaugural Farm Aid benefit concert in September 1985, so Dylan asked if they would back him for the concert. The band agreed instantly and invited him to one of their rehearsals. Petty said, "We played for maybe four hours . . . every kind of song. It was a great time. So we had some more rehearsals and they, too, were fantastic. We all felt comfortable immediately. One thing Bob taught us was not to dwell on one song in rehearsal.

There were nights when I bet we played 50 or 60 songs, which keeps you fresh. I used to go away from rehearsals feeling drained because we would go through a song over and over again, but now I went away from those rehearsals feeling invigorated." There was little repetition and no time to waste grappling with confusion.

After the recycled vibe of *Long After Dark* and the scattered outcome of *Southern Accents*, Petty was wide open to any better situation. He had been hunting for chart-toppers and was mad at himself about it. Zanes said, "A collaboration with an artist like Bob Dylan would put Petty in the company of a man who had set up a very productive shop at some distance from the Billboard charts. Dylan was another teacher who showed up when Petty needed him." Petty would have to moderate his instinct to control everything: "No master plan. As it happened, I was thrown into one of the most artistically fulfilling, one of the lightest in spirit, and certainly one of the most unexpected periods of my life."

The rest of the band members agreed. Said Zanes, "No one in the Heartbreakers went away from working with Dylan without feeling like they'd been to the very best school." They were revitalized by the work. Said Petty, "It was fun again. The funny thing is everybody always talks about what a great songwriter Bob is, so the thing that struck me was how very good a musician he is, too. He hears things right." Their daily rehearsal set lists ran the gamut, but Dylan's approach to teaching the songs was very loose. Howie Epstein recalled that Dylan would simply say, "Here's the song, here's the chords let's do it.' There are no arrangements, we just play." Tench agreed that playing with Dylan "was alternately amazing and frustrating, and sometimes on the same night. I thought it did wonders for playing with the band. It knit us together. Made us looser. You had to improvise." Said Petty, "Onstage, I felt like he had the same spontaneity of a great jazz player."

In short, Dylan taught Petty and the Heartbreakers how to operate more deftly inside a scene of uncertainty: "Among the band members, the Dylan tour registered differently. If they all agree without reserva-tion that the experience took them to the next level as a band, the *not knowing*—not knowing how a song might be played, what key it would be in, what feel—wore on them differently." The band sometimes unleashed these frustrations upon each other, with Stan Lynch particularly getting on Petty's nerves. At one show, nonverbal tensions flared to the point that Petty got so angry he marched offstage.

Dylan came to retrieve him, sulky and silent in the dressing room. After refusing to hear what the fuss was about, he refocused Petty on the enviable guitar task at hand: "He comes in and goes, 'Hey, man, I heard you got mad. Don't be mad. Let's go back and play.' I was so angry, I said, 'Stan gets . . .' But Bob stopped me, said, 'No, no, don't go there. Everything's ok. John Lee Hooker's here. We're going to play with John Lee Hooker. C'mon, you don't want to miss that. Let's go play.'" Lynch had also mightily got into it with Mike Campbell over the guitarist's decision to have his wife and kids along on parts of the tour. Campbell said, "From that point forward, I felt like, 'This guy's not on my side.' I don't remember the words, but the energy was unforgivable."

For Dylan, being backed by a band that could handle the pressure of his spontaneity, however unsteadily, was a burden lifted. Robert Hilburn, rock critic for the *Los Angeles Times*, said that "he kicked off his most ambitious U.S. tour in seven years with the confidence and authority of a man who once again feels secure in his art," and that "Dylan had the lean, hungry look of a man who is finally looking his audience in the eye again."

Hilburn went so far as to say audiences for the True Confessions Tour were witnessing a legend reborn: "Dylan—wearing a loose-fitting white shirt, black leather pants and motorcycle boots—was clearly on the offensive. He displayed the spunk, desire, independence and blazing artistry that characterized him during the '60s when he did more to shape rock than anyone other than Elvis Presley." Despite the Heartbreakers' interpersonal squabbling, said Zanes, "Everyone involved knew that the Dylan tour had heightened the band's capacity to move as a unit, to build something without a blueprint. An already agile group had become something more, a rock-and-roll outfit as fleet-footed as the great studio bands they'd listened to growing up."

Petty said, "I just felt really free for some reason. Everything was clear again. I was so busy focusing on playing well that I forgot about all my problems. I was enjoying music again. I realized that I was worrying too much about pleasing other people or being accepted. I realized that the important thing is to feel good yourself about what you do, and usually if you like it, other people will too." As the Heartbreakers rose to the task before them, Hilburn gave them due credit: "One reason for Dylan's more confident presence is the backing by Tom Petty & the Heartbreakers, the best set of musicians he's worked with since the Band."

It was high praise indeed, and Dylan concurred in his own way: "Tom's finally getting some recognition. That's good. Tom's an excellent songwriter, an excellent musician. People talk about how he sounds a little like Roger McGuinn, but playing with him and seeing what he does to a crowd, I think he's more in the Bob Marley area. He's real good." Dylan's considered compliment is rather telling. Petty had long idolized The Byrds' front man and often got comparisons to McGuinn's twelve-string Rickenbacker jangle, even from McGuinn himself. While conceding that Petty is a fine composer and player, Dylan focused instead on what Petty can do to move an audience. Bob Marley's shows regularly awakened frenzied mob scenes. Even now, the reverence for his legacy still approaches religious fervor. Dylan was saying that Petty had a touch of the preacher in him, had some of that urgently mystical mojo needed to really bring a crowd together.

Underneath this praise was Dylan's doubt about whether he still possessed his own majesty in concert. He recalled being at an all-time career low during that tour, possibly even getting ready to hang it all up. At the October 5, 1987, show in Locarno, Switzerland, Dylan briefly but completely blanked, only to find quite suddenly that the old spark just came flooding back into him. Zanes said Dylan's description of this event "suggests nothing short of a conversion experience." Petty had not suspected that Dylan would be shaken by any self-inflicted comparison to the Heartbreakers:

> In his book [*Chronicles, Volume 1*], he says he was going through a hard time: "Tom was at the top of his game, and I was at the bottom of mine." I didn't know he was so conflicted. It's hard to speak for Bob. But I remember that night he talks about in the book, about going up to the mic to sing and nothing came out of his throat. He took a breath, started again, and it worked. He had some epiphany about staying on the road. I remember that, because I was scared for him: "Uh-oh, something's wrong." Then he sang, and I didn't think about it anymore. It's funny what goes on in people's heads onstage. You don't know. You're just communicating through music.

For Petty, this brief flash of panic read along the lines of his own bouts of laryngitis and stage fright. But Dylan later confided to Hilburn that he was clouded by a much deeper uncertainty:

> When I interviewed Bob in December [of 1997] in Santa Monica, he spoke about regaining his sense of purpose after those hundreds of nights on the Never Ending Tour, and he spoke freely about the disillusionment he had felt for years. "I remember playing shows with Tom Petty and looking out thinking I didn't have that many fans coming to see me," he said. "They were coming to see Tom Petty and the Heartbreakers. I was going on my name for a long time, name and reputation, which was about all I had. I had sort of fallen into an amnesia spell. I didn't feel like I knew who I was on stage.

In his later evaluation of the tour's success, Petty made a fine distinction between performances where the resultant shows sucked versus shows where the performers were grokking around for a way forward: "If he was at the bottom of his game, then the bottom is pretty high, because he really could be riveting on some nights. I did have the sense of that tour that Bob was searching for something . . . maybe searching for the next phase in his career." He easily applied to Dylan the very standard that he had long struggled to apply to himself: "I feel that we had a lot of great nights musically. And maybe because he was in some kind of inner turmoil, he doesn't remember it that way. Maybe I was at the top of my game, but I don't think he was at the bottom of his. I don't think the bottom of his game is that low, anyway. I think he's always good. Maybe, like anyone else, to different degrees on different nights."

This juxtapositioning of a performer's inner doubts with a revolt against them in the form of a successful outer performance of the show is precisely the limit of the absurd, which Camus advised is the necessary precondition for allowing one's openness to doing the most living: "If I convince myself that this life has no other aspect than that of the absurd, if I feel that its whole equilibrium depends on that perpetual opposition between my conscious revolt and the darkness in which it struggles, if I admit that my freedom has no meaning except in relation to its limited fate, then I must say that what counts is not the best living but the most living." After his epiphany with the Heartbreakers in late 1987, Dylan traveled under the banner of the Never Ending Tour in 1988. He understood now that it was all the same tour, going straight into one after another for many years and countless legs.

Said Camus, "Breaking all the records is first and foremost being faced with the world as often as possible. How can that be done without contradictions and without playing on words? For on the one hand the absurd teaches that all experiences are unimportant, and on the other it urges toward the greatest quality of experiences. . . . Being aware of one's life, one's revolt, one's freedom, and to the maximum, is living, and to the maximum." Dylan could find delight in the absurd maximalism of infinite shows, even amid the fatigues of such a long haul, because the increasingly agile Heartbreakers were along for the ride. Said Hilburn,

The Heartbreakers help Dylan in two ways. Where some of the musicians he pulled together for tours had to get to know each other on the road, the Heartbreakers have worked together so long that they move around the stage with the teamwork of the Boston Celtics. Also, Dylan doesn't have the burden of carrying the full load on stage. He can turn things over to Petty, an excellent singer and writer himself, for a couple of 20-minute segments without a loss of momentum. Petty, too, seemed to benefit from the teaming, playing with a joy as refreshing at times as Dylan's.

After the stunningly spirited success of their tour, Dylan and Petty would immediately again seek out a collaborative environment in the interest of pursuing maximum living. They formed a band with other people who need no introduction: George Harrison, Jeff Lynne, and Roy Orbison. The Traveling Wilburys encouraged each superstar to take their turn at the wheel, peaceably backed by the few other performers who understood them. Dylan and Petty essentially found ways to sustain their working relationship from the middle of 1985 through the end of 1990 because they could push each other to do better while paradoxically helping each other mellow out. Petty said, "After a lot of years and a lot of booze, I came to the conclusion that all I can do is try to amuse myself, really. . . . To be honest, we didn't give a shit how we were perceived by other people. That was nothing more than a bunch of guys making an honest attempt at having fun. The Wilburys just refused to take themselves seriously."

Dylan and Petty were keen to tour with the Wilburys, but Harrison wasn't into the idea after Orbison passed away. Still, Dylan continued to reach out to Petty whenever he sensed that the bond forged between the two of them was most needed. Petty especially recalled that when *The Last DJ* came out, "I got a lot of criticism. But I saw it more as a sort of moral play rather than a specifically music-business-oriented thing. Bob Dylan told me that he actually liked the record a lot. He said I shouldn't confuse things that are popular with things that are really good. That was the best review I got." This distinction of the popular versus the good runs parallel to Petty's earlier understanding of the bad show versus the uncertain performer. Of both distinctions, Camus said, "It is essential to die unreconciled."

Perhaps we cannot imagine that Dylan was ever happy. Hilburn said, "I asked him if the word 'happy' might apply to him. He laughed. 'I think that it's hard to find happiness as a whole in anything. The days of tender youth are gone. I think you can be delirious in your youth, but as you get older, things happen.'" Levity is not quite happiness, and the space of a rock star's legacy is perhaps not very conducive to levity anyway. As Hilburn speculated at the opening of the 1986 tour,

> Imagine the odds against writing songs (notably "Like a Rolling Stone" and "Blowin' in the Wind") that become statements of idealism and independence for one generation, and then being able to sing those songs two decades later—a virtual eternity by pop standards—with your own idealism and independence still intact. . . . He remains—in a field that often seems to encourage self-destruction and self-caricature—a man of provocative and unbending artistic will. Yet Dylan wasn't the whole story Sunday. This time, Petty and company were more like co-stars, drawing ovations from the audience with both their endearing, idealistic expressions ("Straight Into Darkness") and their playful new tunes.

In his review of the band's own 1987 headlining tour, suffused with the afterglow of their initial forays with Dylan, Hilburn observed that Petty's "toughened social attitude and more open manner on stage gave the evening a freedom and focus that makes this tour shape up as potentially the Heartbreakers' best in years." There are two slight contradictions embedded there—toughened versus opened, focused versus freed.

Petty had begun to hold himself to these paradoxical standards with far greater ease, refreshed by the new understanding gained through his work with Dylan. He had observed how Dylan maintained his core focus while plagued by doubt, transcended the burden of his calling in rock and roll by way of his authentic connection with the concert crowds. But Petty was hardly just parroting his master. Hilburn said, "Leaning on influences is common in pop. The difference between the best Active bands and most Passive ones is that the influence is incorporated with style rather than left simply intact." An examination of Hilburn's theory of active versus passive bands, and his classification of the Heartbreakers as active, can tell us a lot about how rock stars should navigate the inevitable absurdity of life in their profession. Dylan and Petty were the type to go straight into that darkness.

Absurdity

Camus wondered, "Does the Absurd dictate death?" In the face of that one insurmountable obstacle, which is the sum total of life's constant contradictions, many reasonable people throw in the towel. Or at least they take breaks. In a tour diary entry from 1989, Petty admitted that he was terrible at taking a break: "'We *know* the songs,' said Howie. 'Go rest,' said everyone who's had to deal with me lately. So I'm here resting, I guess. I just walk miles up and down the beach." That is the portrait of a restless person. In 1981, Steve Pond had already summarized a scene that would repeat itself ad infinitum over four decades: "Petty has never made it look easy."

Petty chose not to go gently into that good night of resignation. He instead went straightly into it with a disposition to revolt. Dylan's mystique provided lessons in how to set this standard for himself, and Dylan's hope for what kind of legacy a musician could leave when following this standard was best interpreted by Robert Hilburn. Hilburn served as music editor for the *Los Angeles Times* between 1970 and 2005, where he provided information and passed judgment on nearly everything Tom Petty and the Heartbreakers performed or produced from their debut through their induction into the Rock and Roll Hall of Fame. When the newspaper he called home filed a tribute to Hilburn in 2009, an anecdote concerning the gravity of his Dylan connection provided the lead: "Bob Dylan, dressed for the Grammys in a pewter troubadour's coat and a dandy western tie, arrived backstage to greet the assembled press after winning the album of the year award for 1997, but before the first question he turned to his handlers and asked, 'Is Bob [Hilburn] out there?'"

Hilburn served as an influence as much as an audience. The article continues,

> There were plenty of other nights over his 35-year tenure as *Los Angeles Times* pop music critic when Robert Hilburn became much more than a witness to the scene that he covered for the paper that lands on the doorstep of the music industry. Ken Kesey once said the problem with journalism was that it made a writer more of seismograph than a lightning rod, but he hadn't considered Hilburn's work as a sharp voice of demanding appraisal and something akin to a newsprint conscience for a community that measures merit in spun gold and platinum.

In many ways, the critic had a reputation for being just as ornery as Dylan or Petty. Perhaps that's why the three of them got along, and Hilburn drew quite a bit of his framework for evaluating rock music through the lens of his Dylanology.

Hilburn said, "There are lots of ways to rate rock 'n' roll performers, but Bob Dylan's system makes as much sense as any. Under it, artists fit into one of three categories—the natural performer, who does the best they can do within their limits on stage; the superficial performer, who shouldn't be on stage in the first place because they've got nothing original to tell you; and the supernatural artist, who, in Bob's words, 'is the kind that digs deep and the deeper they go, the more gods they find.'" For his own critical purposes, "There are only two main types of rock bands these days: the Active and the Passive." Superficial, strongly marketed pop performers were designated as passive, while supernatural performers were designated as active. The remaining category of Dylan's triad was collapsed as Hilburn sorted the natural performers into active or passive depending on how they pushed their own limits. Sorting the naturals proved fairly clear-cut for Hilburn. For example, "The Clash is Active; it deals in ideas. Toto is Passive, it deals in sounds."

Hilburn planted Tom Petty and the Heartbreakers squarely in the active bands category: "Passive bands can do enticing work (Boston's 'More Than a Feeling'), but the artistic heartbeat of rock rests with the more challenging Active outfits: Bruce Springsteen, Elvis Costello, Tom Petty, Talking Heads, Patti Smith, the Cars, Devo and the Clash," he wrote in 1979. "While they welcome sales, the primary intent of Active rockers is to say something, and to say it with the individuality that is at the base of all worthwhile art." "I guess you just call it non-gimmick rock," Petty told Hilburn in 1987, "which is what we've always tried to do." Hilburn appreciated that "there isn't always just one interpretation. The aim is to make you feel and consider: get involved."

As opposed to this intensely thoughtful connection active bands sought to construct with their audience, "the technique of Passive outfits like Toto, Boston, Foreigner, Kansas and Styx is to reduce all challenge and mystery so that a listener can absorb the music as easily as the handsome photos in a glossy coffee-table book." To Hilburn, bands like this failed on all three of the key levels identified by Camus: "I draw from the absurd three consequences, which are my revolt, my freedom, and my passion. By the mere activity of consciousness I transform into a rule of life what was an invitation to death—and I refuse suicide." Passive bands are unconscious ones—suicidal bands that tend to burn themselves out with despair over the nothingness of their meaningless, corporate-run careers.

Hilburn used his critical influence to garner more attention on behalf of active bands. Said his colleague Geoff Boucher, "His early championing led to breakthroughs for artists such as Elton John, Bruce Springsteen, Gram Parsons, Tom Petty and the Heartbreakers, U2, N.W.A,

Rage Against the Machine, Nine Inch Nails, Eminem, Alicia Keys and the White Stripes. Hilburn was notorious for his persistent advocacy for some artists." His insistent favoring of these active musicians garnered the critic something of a reputation: "The joke in the newsroom was that he loved to celebrate the four 'Bs,' which stood for Bruce, Bob Dylan, Bono and Bruce again—but it was his negative reviews that stuck in the memory of his subjects."

To Petty's credit, Hilburn found him a worthwhile foil for Springsteen, saying in 1979, "Springsteen's music may rely on teen images of fast cars, rebellious nights and sexual desire, but his songs are too well crafted to be limited to a single age group. At their best, the songs strike at any force that stands between an individual and his legitimate aspirations. The same is true of Petty's music. The imagery in the Los Angeles–based rocker's songs isn't as stylized as it is in Springsteen's, but the impact is often just as jolting." Petty likewise credited Hilburn:

> The critic at the *L.A. Times*, Robert Hilburn, wrote a very nice review of us. He'd actually written about the album prior to that and given it a so-so review. Then he wrote a second one saying that he was wrong, that our record is actually really great. In a rare and wonderful instance of critical humility—we need all of that we can get, right?—he wrote a second review because he changed his mind. Then he did an interview with me, a nice piece. That got us a weeklong stand at the Whisky. By the time the shows happened, we were seeing lines around the block.

Hilburn's description of the band in 1977 already identified the hallmarks of their legacy:

> Petty and the Heartbreakers is a classic rock 'n' roll band, one whose sound hasn't been polluted by the excesses so common in today's recycled pop scene. There's a purity in the group's music that combines the shadowy, late-night compulsion of the Rolling Stones' *Exile on Main Street* with the classic American immediacy that can be traced back to Elvis and Eddie Cochran. The tone is urgent, defiant, desperate. Rather

than overstate, his music leaves room for the imagination. His themes touch on familiar rock experiences but are free of the usual calculation and pretense. The emotion comes across as genuine and gripping.

Hilburn understood the band to be active—mythic yet authentic, foreboding yet inviting, both shadowy and pure. Petty told Hilburn at that time, "A record has to be true. It has to be real. That's what I look for, the believability."

The following year, Hilburn observed how Petty's devotion to the concertgoing experience was always returned to him in kind by his audience, even as the gigs grew into larger venues with much bigger crowds: "He and the Heartbreakers band deal in a classic rock style so powerful and pure you'd think they'd stumbled across some long-lost formula. Most importantly, Petty connects with his audiences. When the blond, 25-year-old singer-guitarist walked on stage with the Heartbreakers Monday night at the sold-out Santa Monica Civic, the audience erupted with a shrieking, cheering ovation normally reserved for rock's most established figures." All of the Heartbreakers treated this responsibility to their live audiences seriously, as demonstrated in the care they took to determine a set list. Said Campbell, "It's complicated now because we've been around for so long that we can't even fit all the hits in the show, and if we try to put anything new in, or any cover, that means a hit comes off. . . . So our challenge is, no matter what we put in there, to win them over in spite of not hearing the song they wanted."

Tench agreed that the band was willing to work for their audience connection, with a caveat about self-fulfillment: "It's almost wrong of you not to play [the hits], but you also have to do something for yourself and your fans that aren't just casual fans. At our show, the bulk of the fans want to hear 20 or 30 of our songs, and it sacrifices stuff that I want to play." Petty could also be resentful about having to pack the set list full of hits. For example, when the Replacements were opening for the band in 1989, bassist Tommy Stinson wanted to know if "Breakdown" was going to be on their set list, and Petty rolled his eyes: "Yeah, we still do that. I think I'll know we're really doing OK when I don't have to do that song anymore. . . . Why don't you do the song and then we won't have to?"

When the audience was invested in a particular hit, the Heartbreakers considered whether to oblige by playing it to cultivate their longevity, as opposed to the promotional machine's demand for making new hits while in the studio. An active band trusts their fans a great deal and trusts their record label very little. As early as 1978, just two years after their debut, Petty viewed any conflict with the business side of their work as an insult to the Heartbreakers' intellect: "I told all the lawyers that I had made a living a long time before I made records, and if I couldn't get a fair deal, I just wouldn't record anymore. I meant it. I was fed up. We were being treated like we were stupid. We are not stupid."

Petty could zoom out on a situation and distance himself from insult, whether it was corporate feedback or a negative review. But he also insisted on moderation when accepting praise because it was fundamentally at odds with the core standard of his personal intention: "Sometimes I feel really gracious. Everything is really good, the world is so wonderful. It doesn't last very long. I'm always pissed off at something again. It's the best position for observing. You see all these groups get to the top, get too content and then blow it with bad music. Our intention is to stay pissed off." He was not willing to entertain contentment because it would breed that same passivity criticized by Hilburn.

Just as Dylan engaged in the Never Ending Tour , this is how Petty enacted the endless revolt required by Camus:

> The theme of permanent revolution is thus carried into individual experience. Living is keeping the absurd alive. Keeping it alive is, above all, contemplating it. Unlike Eurydice, the absurd dies only when we turn away from it. One of the only coherent philosophical positions is thus revolt. It is a constant confrontation between man and his own obscurity. It is an insistence upon an impossible transparency. It chal-

lenges the world anew every second. . . . That revolt is the certainty of a crushing fate, without the resignation that ought to accompany it.

Petty acknowledged absurdity and even identified it as a source of satisfaction: "I don't think I've been any happier than I am today, which isn't the same as saying that I'm at peace with the world." He showed not only that a defiant attitude and happiness are not mutually exclusive but also that such a stance is in fact the necessary precondition for any happiness. The Heartbreakers were not at peace, not a passive outfit—they were working, saying something despite the existential odds of it landing in any useful way. The joy of being an active band is the same joy Camus defined for Sisyphus, who is stuck endlessly pushing his rock back up the hill: "One always finds one's burden again. But Sisyphus teaches the higher fidelity that negates the gods and raises rocks. He too concludes that all is well. This universe henceforth without a master seems to him neither sterile nor futile. Each atom of that stone, each mineral flake of that night filled mountain, in itself forms a world. The struggle itself toward the heights is enough to fill a man's heart. One must imagine Sisyphus happy."

We can therefore say that all was well for the Heartbreakers as long as Petty was not at peace. The revolt he waged reveals the nuanced fulfillment of those who are constantly working, and it did not sour him on life: "I don't think I'm a bitter old man. I'm an optimist. I believe in the human spirit. I believe we can overcome a lot of things. But it gets harder and harder, with the way things are. I'd love to say, 'Shit is so much better now.' But it was better then." He could simultaneously laugh about how the differences we perceive between "then" and "now" matter an absurdly little amount, and how the work we do is ultimately not going to be much about whatever we think it's about at the time we're doing it. For example, a fan once approached Petty on the street to praise *Echo*, which is the album Petty most notoriously loathed. Almost twenty years after the album was made, Petty summed up the fan encounter to a reporter by offering, "Well, see? Things can work out even when you don't realize it. You know?"

In the early days of his music career, Petty's existential angst often couldn't be channeled in such an easygoing manner. The band sometimes confused authenticity with anger. During their 1981 practices, Lynch said, "The cat's just pissed. I see it every time I play with him. He's real passionate. Even in rehearsal, he'll come stompin' in. He means it." The fans followed suit. In response to reports on the band's battle with MCA in 1981, a kid wrote in to *Rolling Stone* simply to declare, "Tom Petty is on our side." Petty told Hilburn: "I was in this defiant mood. I wasn't so conscious of it then, but I can look back and see what was happening. I find that's true a lot. It takes some time usually before you fully understand what's going on in a song—or maybe what led up to it."

This is especially true of the "dark period" represented by *Long After Dark*. Only three tracks from this album made it into the top fifty list of Petty tunes drawn up by *Rolling Stone*. "Change of Heart" ranks twenty-first and "You Got Lucky" ranks twenty-third. "Straight Into Darkness" ranks twenty-eighth. Although Hilburn conceded that *Long After Dark* "was viewed as a disappointment in several quarters," he nevertheless felt that the album "featured some of [Petty's] most impressive lyrics." He would later elaborate on how the album portrayed Petty's growth as a songwriter: "Petty's best early songs, including 'American Girl' and 'Listen to Her Heart,' were usually framed in romantic terms, but spoke about desire and faith in ways that went beyond boy/girl relationships. Increasingly, however, Petty began to address those subjects more directly. Ironically, *Long After Dark* contained some of his best songs in this vein, notably 'Straight Into Darkness.' But there was a perception that Petty was standing still because the arrangements on record seemed to sound the same."

Hilburn's original review of *Long After Dark* appeared in the *Sarasota Herald-Tribune* on November 6, 1982, a handful of days after Petty's thirty-second birthday. The headline was "Petty Gets His Message Across"—ironic, given that Petty was lost in the undertow of his absurd condition at the time and couldn't figure out what the album was saying. The first sentence of the review cited a paradox that becomes instantly hilarious in the context of Camus, promising that the album was "a textbook example of how to have your cake in rock and eat it too." Having the cake refers to "Petty's ability to weave meaningful themes" like all great active bands, and eating the cake too refers to the album's "highly commercial framework," which is more indicative of a passive band. The critic stated their formula explicitly: "The secret is putting your message into the popular or accepted language of rock so that passive, mainstream fans can enjoy the music on a casual level while other, more active fans can appreciate it on a deeper level. Though most of the collection's lively, engaging songs deal with the search for romance, it is more rewarding to view the lyrics as statements about maintaining integrity of your dreams, whether they involve career or relationships."

Contrary to radio's focus on "Change of Heart" or MTV's focus on "You Got Lucky," either of which the record company was willing to promote as a single, Hilburn used the space of his review to drill down on "Straight Into Darkness," declaring it "the album's central song." He said the song "not only illustrates the twin appeal of Petty's music, but also demonstrates why this album is his most fully satisfying work." For passive listeners, the song "is on the surface a melancholy song about falling in and out of love," but for an active audience, "it also is a pledge to rally against disillusionment." Hilburn comprehended the song in its fullest association with Camus's existential crisis: "Early in the song, Petty equates the darkness observed late at night from the window of a 747 with the anxious uncertainty that many now feel when assessing the state of the American Dream. But Petty rejects the temptation to temper his own dreams."

Hilburn then quoted the bridge verse and the first two lines of the chorus, identifying the message as "deeper" and "more convincing" than mere idealism. He said this song is the highlight of what the album was able to accomplish, and tossed in another undercurrent of comparison to Springsteen: "The advances in *Long After Dark* are reflected in the increased sophistication of his lyrics. It is clear that the same spirit is behind 'Listen to Her Heart' and 'Straight Into Darkness,' but there is a darker, more penetrating edge to the latter song that the younger Petty probably was not capable of four years ago." The critic returned to both the song and to Springsteen in his final conclusion: "Petty's ability to move from the primitive rock celebration of 'Same Old You' to the haunting philosophical refinement of 'Straight Into Darkness' enables him to operate on rock's two most powerful plains. He does not exhibit in *Long After Dark* the bold sociocultural redirection of Springsteen's *Nebraska*. The core of the album, however, suggests a parallel passion."

Perhaps a song of "haunting philosophical refinement" is not the most obvious choice when it comes time to make a set list. Hilburn agreed in his 1985 review of the Heartbreakers in concert, when they were touring *Southern Accents*:

> For all its crowd-pleasing vigor, however, the concert failed to resolve a problem that has been nagging Petty ever since his hugely successful *Damn the Torpedoes* album in 1979: the suspicion that this slender, Florida-born rocker has peaked. That view is supported by the sales charts. . . . While much of the *Hard Promises* and, especially, *Long After Dark* albums did sound similar to Petty's earlier work, there was an increased subtlety and sophistication in Petty's lyrics, which are chiefly uplifting expressions about innocence and desire. The problem is that sophistication isn't what much of Petty's *Torpedoes* audience wanted. They were eager for more of the hard-edged, ringing-guitar rockers. So, here was a man who was getting better as a writer—yet finding a large part of his audience is slipping away.

That right there is one of absurdity's paradoxes. Petty told Hilburn the trade-offs of being an active band were totally worth it, that the intentionality of his newly narrowing mob scene suited him just fine: "I feel a little restricted with love songs now. At one time I didn't, but I just think there is too much going on to ignore it, and I think Live Aid showed us the power that musicians have now. To me, Live Aid was a pretty dreadful show if you had to take it on musical content alone, but the intent was fantastic. Sure, some people are saying we're having too many benefits in rock, but I'd much rather see us [guilty of] that than the other way." Above all, Petty felt it was important to keep working to interrogate. He told Hilburn, "As a songwriter, the best thing I can achieve is to get someone to think about things. I can't give them the answers."

On *Long After Dark*, Petty was definitely thinking about things, even if those things ultimately remained cloudy or undefined. He felt that there was no message to get across, and yet, according to the absurd, simply to posit the existence of this type of darkness is in itself a valid and rather confrontational message. Camus said, "Just as one does or does not kill oneself, it seems that there are but two philosophical solutions, either yes or no. This would be too easy. But allowance must be made for those who, without concluding, continue questioning."

To continue questioning is to go straight into darkness, and that is Petty's legacy. The *Long After Dark* album can be considered lame only if Petty's catalog is evaluated according to the standards for a passive band. To judge his work instead by the standards of an active band, "Straight Into Darkness" may be one of the most valuable songs Petty ever wrote. Hilburn was still referencing it twenty years later, in 2002, because it "spoke about the tensions of trying to keep your spirits up when everything around you is in turmoil"—a mob scene that simply never goes out of style.

Even after two decades, Petty told Hilburn he couldn't comprehend why "Straight Into Darkness" doesn't get more credit: "I like that song a lot. I don't know why it was never put out as a single. Maybe it was just a little too dark. There were a lot of tensions going on around me and I was trying to combat the pessimism. I wanted to say that love is the great redeemer. We played it quite a bit live, and it always went over well." Said Hilburn,

> Rock fans adopt heroes and discard them in ways that are both careless and profoundly heartfelt. This compulsive turnover is wholly correct in terms of rock's instinctive, populist nature, but it can lead to bad judgments when measuring the 30-plus year history of rock. Like all art forms, rock is evolutionary, one generation of artists building upon the contributions of earlier generations. Some of the albums of the last 10 years may actually prove more influential than the works—like *Sgt. Pepper's* and *Exile*—that are now considered essential, but it is going to take time for them to prove their case.

Born in 1950, Petty was "as old as rock & roll itself." *Long After Dark* is now forty years old. Petty himself turned forty just as he began studio sessions for *Into the Great Wide Open*, in 1991. Taking stock of his life's work at that point, he said,

> It's tough when you look in the mirror and go, "Shit, I'm an old guy." But the night I turned 40, there was a big party for me, so I was surrounded by friends. And I'm glad I turned 40 at a good time in my life. I didn't go through it a few years ago, when I was feeling like a failure at everything. Like the song says, "I was so much older then, I'm younger than that now." And I listen to the new album and I feel so good, because it's not a cheap shot. It's not a bunch of old assholes trying to take your money. In a way I'm really upbeat about turning 40. I feel like, "Well, I'm still here, you know." And that's more than some people can say. I'm still here, and I'm still doing something.

In 1977, Petty told Hilburn that the standard that he set for himself was to still be working at saying something: "Getting recognized does a real strange thing. The more people hear about you the more chances they're gonna have a chip on their shoulder and say, 'Man, he'd really better deliver.' Our only line of attack is we're gonna keep doing what we've been doing. At least it's good to feel we're not still just beating our heads against the wall. We've got people listening now." By 1985, when the standards for passive bands seemed to have really got a stranglehold on rock and roll, Petty affirmed to Hilburn what it means to stay pissed off: "I hate being expected to do anything. It's good to stir the pot a little."

For Camus, "That revolt gives life its value. Spread out over the whole length of a life, it restores its majesty to that life. To a man devoid of blinders, there is no finer sight than that of intelligence at grips with a reality that transcends it. . . . That discipline that the mind imposes on itself, that will conjured up out of nothing, that face-to-face struggle have something exceptional about them." Hilburn agreed that this band did not bow down before the challenge of a rock and roll existence, that their work earned a place among exceptional gods. Said Hilburn, "Rather than tailor his style to better fit critical or commercial trends, the singer-songwriter and his band the Heartbreakers have remained true, in themes and presentation, to the basic rock and roll tradition that they learned from the records of such classic figures as Elvis Presley, the Beatles, the Rolling Stones, the Byrds and Bob Dylan." No song more fully attests to the existential dilemma, or more completely underscores Tom Petty's legacy in negotiating it, than "Straight Into Darkness."

Acknowledgments

This book has been sitting inside of me for a very long while. I'm grateful to Nell Minnow and Miniver Press for bringing it out to the public for the first time, and equally grateful to the team at University of Georgia Press for giving it a second life—especially Jordan Stepp and Beth Snead. Parts of the Atlanta essay first appeared in *Atlanta INtown*, with thanks due to Collin Kelly. Parts of the Introduction essay first appeared in *PopMatters*, with thanks due to Karen Zarker. My Canadian Pettyhead pal from the "Mine" essay in the Mob Scene section, Claire Dixon Wilson, provided useful feedback on a draft of this manuscript. Most of whatever I do is impossible without Mindy agreeing to push her own rock up the same mountain as I push mine. And, of course, I'm indebted to Tom Petty and the Heartbreakers.

Notes

INTRODUCTION

3 "If this myth is tragic . . ." ✦ Albert Camus, *The Myth of Sisyphus and Other Essays*, trans. Justin O'Brien (New York: Alfred A. Knopf; rpt., New York: Vintage, 1991), 23. Originally published in France as *Le Mythe de Sisyphe* by Librairie Gallimard, 1942.

4 "I thought the world of . . ." ✦ Kory Grow and Andy Greene, "Tom Petty, Rock Icon Who Led the Heartbreakers, Dead at 66," *Rolling Stone*, October 2, 2017, https://www.rollingstone.com/music/music-news/tom-petty-rock-icon-who-led-the-heartbreakers-dead-at-66-197469/.

ALBUM CONTEXT: UP UNTIL 1981

11 "The lawsuit revealed something . . ." ✦ Warren Zanes, *Petty: The Biography* (New York: Henry Holt, 2015), 142.

11 "On that album, we came . . ." ✦ Paul Zollo, *Conversations with Tom Petty* (New York: Omnibus, 2005), 64.

12 "If the first two records . . ." ✦ Zanes, *Petty*, 146.

12 "In the studio it could . . ." ✦ Zollo, *Conversations with Tom Petty*, 49.

12 "Live, Stan was a great drummer . . ." ✦ Zanes, *Petty*, 144–145.

12 "*really* tough on Stan . . ." ✦ Zollo, *Conversations with Tom Petty*, 64.

12 "just couldn't understand why Stan . . ." ✦ Zanes, *Petty*, 143.

12 "I remember taking a *day* . . ." ✦ Zollo, *Conversations with Tom Petty*, 64.

12 "it's the only time I've walked out . . ." ✦ Zanes, *Petty*, 146.

13 "was already drifting away . . ." ✦ Zanes, *Petty*, 161.

13 "is when this became a job . . ." ✦ Zollo, *Conversations with Tom Petty*, 73.

13 "We always frowned on people . . ." ✦ Peter Bogdanovich, *Tom Petty and the Heartbreakers: Runnin' Down a Dream*, ed. Warren Zanes (San Fransisco, Calif.: Chronicle, 2007), 79.

13 "*Hard Promises* was an extreme example . . ." ✦ Tom Petty and the Heartbreakers, *Playback*, liner notes by Bill Flanagan, MCA Records, 1995.

13 "*Hard Promises* had represented something . . ." ✦ Tom Petty and the Heartbreakers, *Playback*, liner notes.

13 "the Dylan thing" ✦ Zanes, *Petty*, 163.

14 "I was proud that I . . ." ✦ Zollo, *Conversations with Tom Petty*, 73.

14 "That really affected me mentally . . ." ✦ Zollo, *Conversations with Tom Petty*, 73.

ALBUM CONTEXT: MAKING THE ALBUM

16 "stole" ✦ Paul Zollo, *Conversations with Tom Petty* (New York: Omnibus, 2005), 76.

16 "I've told this story . . ." ✦ Warren Zanes, *Petty: The Biography* (New York: Henry Holt, 2015), 167.

16 "No one in or around the band . . ." ✦ Zanes, *Petty*, 167.

16–17 "The way we'd talk about . . ." ✦ Zanes, *Petty*, 167.

17 "[Ron] was very sincere . . ." ✦ Zollo, *Conversations with Tom Petty*, 76.

17 "A vacancy in the band . . ." ✦ Zanes, *Petty*, 169.

17 "With Blair gone, there was . . ." ✦ Zanes, *Petty*, 170.

17 "Epstein had two qualities . . ." ✦ Tom Petty and the Heartbreakers, *Playback*, liner notes by Bill Flanagan, MCA Records, 1995.

17 "Howie came in and was . . ." ✦ Andrea M. Rotondo, *Tom Petty: Rock 'n' Roll Guardian* (New York: Overlook Omnibus, 2014), 216–217.

17 "If somebody else comes up . . ." ✦ Tom Petty and the Heartbreakers, *Playback*, liner notes.

18 "They went through the rectum . . ." ✦ Zanes, *Petty*, 179.

18 "Nobody was entirely satisfied . . ." ✦ Tom Petty and the Heartbreakers, *Playback*, liner notes.

18 "There were songs being left . . ." ✦ Zollo, *Conversations with Tom Petty*, 80, 82.

18 "Iovine felt I had gone too far . . ." ✦ Tom Petty and the Heartbreakers, *Playback*, liner notes.

18–19 "I didn't see them as . . ." ✦ Zollo, *Conversations with Tom Petty*, 82.

19 "I really think Iovine wanted . . ." ✦ Zollo, *Conversations with Tom Petty*, 82.

19 "felt that he had allowed . . ." ✦ Tom Petty and the Heartbreakers, *Playback*, liner notes.

19 "I don't know if our best . . ." ✦ Zollo, *Conversations with Tom Petty*, 218.

19 "I felt that we were . . ." ✦ Tom Petty and the Heartbreakers, *Playback*, liner notes.

19 "It was a tough record . . ." ✦ Zollo, *Conversations with Tom Petty*, 81.

19 "I don't know how many . . ." ✦ Rotondo, *Tom Petty*, 251.

20 "The Everly Brothers songs aren't . . ." ✦ Tom Petty and the Heartbreakers, *Playback*, liner notes.

20 "It's almost Buddy Holly–ish, or . . ." ✦ Tom Petty and the Heartbreakers, *Playback*, liner notes.

ALBUM CONTEXT: PROMOTING THE ALBUM

22 "his years living inside . . ." ✦ Warren Zanes, *Petty: The Biography* (New York: Henry Holt, 2015), 150.

22 "write the songs, go . . ." ✦ Zanes, *Petty*, 150.

22–23 "For months, the schedule was . . ." ✦ Steve Pond, "The Hard Way," *Rolling Stone*, July 23, 1981.

23 "It happens that the stage . . ." ✦ Albert Camus, *The Myth of Sisyphus and Other Essays*, trans. Justin O'Brien (New York: Alfred A. Knopf, 1955; rpt., New York: Vintage, 1991), 5. Originally published in France as *Le Mythe de Sisyphe* by Librairie Gallimard, 1942.

23 "This divorce between . . ." ✦ Camus, *Myth of Sisyphus*, 2.

23–24 "judging whether life is . . ." ✦ Camus, *Myth of Sisyphus*, 1.

24 "an act like this is . . ." ✦ Camus, *Myth of Sisyphus*, 2.

24 "At this point in his . . ." ✦ Camus, *Myth of Sisyphus*, 10.

24 "From the moment absurdity . . ." ✦ Camus, *Myth of Sisyphus*, 8.

24 "almost ceaseless movement between writing . . ." ✦ Zanes, *Petty*, 140.

24–25 "a matter of Petty wanting . . ." ✦ Zanes, *Petty*, 178.

25 "If the descent is thus . . ." ✦ Camus, *Myth of Sisyphus*, 24.

25 "There is no sun without . . ." ✦ Camus, *Myth of Sisyphus*, 24.

25 "One does not discover the . . ." ✦ Camus, *Myth of Sisyphus*, 24.

25 "I really thought it might . . ." ✦ Zanes, *Petty*, 179.

25 "really, really good song . . ." ✦ Peter Bogdanovich, *Tom Petty and the Heart-breakers: Runnin' Down a Dream*, ed. Warren Zanes (San Francisco, Calif.: Chronicle, 2007), 101.

25 "I think it's a good . . ." ✦ Bogdanovich, *Tom Petty and the Heartbreakers*, 101.

25–26 "The Heartbreakers got on a . . ." ✦ Zanes, *Petty*, 180.

26 "On the *Long After Dark* tour. . ." ✦ Zanes, *Petty*, 188.

26 "I started to take it . . ." ✦ Andrea M. Rotondo, *Tom Petty: Rock 'n' Roll Guardian* (New York: Overlook Omnibus, 2014), 119–120.

26 "the dark period" ✦ Zanes, *Petty*, 181.

26 "In a man's attachment . . ." ✦ Camus, *Myth of Sisyphus*, 3.

26 "Killing yourself amounts to confessing . . ." ✦ Camus, *Myth of Sisyphus*, 2.

26 "in order to keep alive . . ." ✦ Camus, *Myth of Sisyphus*, 19.

26 "the most misunderstood song . . ." ✦ Bill Flanagan, *Written in My Soul* (Chicago, Ill.: Contemporary, 1986), qtd. in Nick Thomas, *Tom Petty: An American Rock and Roll Story* (Green, Ohio: Guardian Express Media, 2014), 115.

27 "He'd sit there and spend . . ." ✦ Zanes, *Petty*, 66.

27 "Then in 1981, for *Hard Promises* . . ." ✦ Craig Marks and Rob Tannenbaum, *I Want My MTV: The Uncensored Story of the Music Video Revolution* (New York: Penguin, 2011), 37.

27 "'You Got Lucky' was a . . ." ✦ Marks and Tannenbaum, *I Want My MTV*, 106.

27 "it really changed everything. No . . ." ✦ Paul Zollo, *Conversations with Tom Petty* (New York: Omnibus, 2005), 83.

27 "that video was terrific fun . . ." ✦ Marks and Tannenbaum, *I Want My MTV*, 106.

28 "There was a lot of coke . . ." ✦ Marks and Tannenbaum, *I Want My MTV*, 272.

28 "He is, as much through . . ." ♦ Camus, *Myth of Sisyphus*, 23.

28 "I didn't much like making . . ." ♦ Marks and Tannenbaum, *I Want My MTV*, 95.

28 "We got 90 percent of . . ." ♦ Marks and Tannenbaum, *I Want My MTV*, 242.

28 "Sykes knew how to build . . ." ♦ Marks and Tannenbaum, *I Want My MTV*, 138.

28 "Les [Garland] and Sykes managed . . ." ♦ Marks and Tannenbaum, *I Want My MTV*, 138.

28–29 "I never thought it was fair . . ." ♦ Marks and Tannenbaum, *I Want My MTV*, 242.

29 "MTV—I could tell . . ." ♦ David Fricke, "It's Good to Be the King," *Rolling Stone*, December 10, 2009.

29 "The theme of the irrational . . ." ♦ Camus, *Myth of Sisyphus*, 17.

29 "We didn't go for the . . ." ♦ Marks and Tannenbaum, *I Want My MTV*, 307.

29 "at last man will again . . ." ♦ Camus, *Myth of Sisyphus*, 18.

30 "It is probably true that . . ." ♦ Camus, *Myth of Sisyphus*, 4.

SONG COMPOSITION: ARRANGEMENT

37 "Wherever you turned there were . . ." ♦ Rod McShane, "Tom Petty on the Road: This Is How It Feels," *Rolling Stone*, August 1977.

37 "The stuff that got me . . ." ♦ David Hunter, "Mike Campbell: Anything That's Rock 'n' Roll," June 1999, qtd. in Nick Thomas, *Tom Petty: An American Rock and Roll Story* (Green, Ohio: Guardian Express Media, 2014), 30–31.

37 "Campbell's style lies somewhere between . . ." ♦ Andrea M. Rotondo, *Tom Petty: Rock 'n' Roll Guardian* (New York: Overlook Omnibus, 2014), 180.

37–38 "His way of playing the guitar . . ." ♦ Jas Obrecht, "Mike Campbell with the Heartbreakers," *Guitar Player*, August 1986.

38 "Jimmy Iovine told me . . ." ♦ Blair Jackson, "Tom Petty's Victory," *BAM*, December 1979.

38 "bass and drums is the . . ." ♦ Warren Zanes, *Petty: The Biography* (New York: Henry Holt, 2015), 90.

38 "We got there only through . . ." ✦ Peter Bogdanovich, *Tom Petty and the Heartbreakers: Runnin' Down a Dream*, ed. Warren Zanes (San Francisco, Calif.: Chronicle, 2007), 70.

38–39 "You can hear that Benmont . . ." ✦ Zanes, *Petty*, 81.

39 "Ben's 'On the Street' was . . ." ✦ Zanes, *Petty*, 82.

39 "certainly conveys just how artfully . . ." ✦ Zanes, *Petty*, 97.

39 "We just played it once . . ." ✦ Paul Zollo, *Conversations with Tom Petty* (New York: Omnibus, 2005), 222.

39 "Benmont was really angry about . . ." ✦ Zollo, *Conversations with Tom Petty*, 219.

39 "I remember it really came . . ." ✦ Zollo, *Conversations with Tom Petty*, 221.

39 "We were trying to do it . . ." ✦ Zollo, *Conversations with Tom Petty*, 221.

40 "working with a group" ✦ Zollo, *Conversations with Tom Petty*, 221.

40–41 "It's as if, on *Torpedoes* . . ." ✦ Rotondo, *Tom Petty*, 111.

41 "Instead of finding glory . . ." ✦ Rotondo, *Tom Petty*, 105.

41 "As formidable a success as . . ." ✦ Rotondo, *Tom Petty*, 108.

41 "In the past, Petty had . . ." ✦ Nick Thomas, *Tom Petty: An American Rock and Roll Story* (Green, Ohio: Guardian Express Media, 2014), 168–169.

41 "With 'American Girl,' he brought . . ." ✦ Zanes, *Petty*, 111.

45 "That's the kind of band . . ." ✦ Zollo, *Conversations with Tom Petty*, 222.

SONG LYRICS: VERSE I

49 "There's times I'll hear a . . ." ✦ Richard Hogan, "Tom Petty Makes 'Hard Promises' to Rock & Roll," *Circus*, August 31, 1981.

49 "It was kind of like . . ." ✦ Sylvie Simmons, "Moonlighting," *Raw*, June 14, 1989.

49 "I'm real good with ambiguity . . ." ✦ Alan di Perna, "Tom Petty: American Boy," *Pulse*, April 1999.

50 "I was always the man . . ." ✦ Paul Zollo, *Conversations with Tom Petty* (New York: Omnibus, 2005), 202.

50 "The 'American Girl' is just . . ." ✦ Andrea M. Rotondo, *Tom Petty: Rock 'n' Roll Guardian* (New York: Overlook Omnibus, 2014), 71.

53 "who had been back for . . ." ✦ Zollo, *Conversations with Tom Petty*, 217.

SONG LYRICS: VERSE 2

55 "England has always been Mecca . . ." ✦ Andrea M. Rotondo, *Tom Petty: Rock 'n' Roll Guardian* (New York: Overlook Omnibus, 2014), 142.

55 "the home of our heroes" ✦ Paul Zollo, *Conversations with Tom Petty* (New York: Omnibus Press, 2005), 55.

55 "We sat around all day . . ." ✦ Rotondo, *Tom Petty*, 44.

56 "it was just a windstorm . . ." ✦ Rotondo, *Tom Petty*, 55.

56 "It was an amazing time . . ." ✦ Peter Bogdanovich, *Tom Petty and the Heartbreakers: Runnin' Down a Dream*, ed. Warren Zanes (San Francisco, Calif.: Chronicle, 2007), 54.

56 "there were riots fifteen minutes . . ." ✦ Stephen Peeples, "Tom Petty and the Heartbreakers: Hogtown Boy Makes Good," *Rock around the World*, October 9, 1977.

56 "one of the most in-demand bands . . ." ✦ "More Than a Pretty Face," *Melody Maker*, 1977.

56 "the UK seemed to get . . ." ✦ Rotondo, *Tom Petty*, 77.

56 "By the time we left . . ." ✦ Melinda Newman, "Tom Petty: A Portrait of the Artist," *Billboard*, December 3, 2005.

56–57 "Of everything we've done . . ." ✦ Jaan Uhelszki, "Tom Petty: Won't Back Down," *Uncut*, June 2012.

57 "LA is not nearly as bad . . ." ✦ Steve Morse, "Tom Petty: A Survivor," *Boston Globe*, March 24, 1983.

57 "I think with the last . . ." ✦ Robert Palmer, "A New Album by Petty and the Heartbreakers," *New York Times*, March 25, 1985.

SONG LYRICS: CHORUS I

60 "I'm certainly not trying to . . ." ✦ Andrea M. Rotondo, *Tom Petty: Rock 'n' Roll Guardian* (New York: Overlook Omnibus, 2014), 233.

61 "the darkest period of my . . ." ✦ Rotondo, *Tom Petty*, 193.

61 "You can file things like . . ." ✦ Peter Bogdanovich, *Tom Petty and the Heartbreakers: Runnin' Down a Dream*, ed. Warren Zanes (San Francisco, Calif.: Chronicle, 2007), 79.

61–62 "[The album] was very angry . . ." ✦ Tom Petty and the Heartbreakers, *Playback*, liner notes by Bill Flanagan, MCA Records, 1995.

62 "My feeling is that you'll . . ." ✦ Bogdanovich, *Tom Petty and the Heartbreakers*, 98.

62 "It's about waiting for your dreams . . ." ✦ Robert Hilburn, "No Backing Down," *Los Angeles Times*, March 15, 2002.

63 "Phrasing is really important . . ." ✦ Paul Zollo, *Conversations with Tom Petty* (New York: Omnibus, 2005), 198.

63 "If I don't believe it . . ." ✦ Rotondo, *Tom Petty*, 232.

63 "If there's one thing I know . . ." ✦ Rotondo, *Tom Petty*, 93.

63 "kind of a play on . . ." ✦ Zollo, *Conversations with Tom Petty*, 219.

63–64 "That song frightened me when . . ." ✦ Rotondo, *Tom Petty*, 155–156.

64 "We've probably been the most . . ." ✦ Steve Morse, "Tom Petty: A Survivor," *Boston Globe*, March 24, 1983.

64 "I'm not one of those people . . ." ✦ Rotondo, *Tom Petty*, 232.

64 "That's kinda my theory of life . . ." ✦ Rotondo, *Tom Petty*, 188.

64 "straight jobs" ✦ Rotondo, *Tom Petty*, 32.

65 "I'm trying to learn . . ." ✦ Rotondo, *Tom Petty*, 187.

65 "You're a good man to . . ." ✦ Bogdanovich, *Tom Petty and the Heartbreakers*, 207.

65 "Me? I like whatever approach . . ." ✦ Bogdanovich, *Tom Petty and the Heartbreakers*, 175.

66 "There is a certain satisfaction . . ." ✦ Rotondo, *Tom Petty*, 99.

66 "When I hear *Long After Dark* . . ." ✦ Rotondo, *Tom Petty*, 118.

SONG LYRICS: BRIDGE VERSE

68 "We always call it . . ." ✦ Paul Zollo, *Conversations with Tom Petty* (New York: Omnibus, 2005), 200.

68 "It's the part of the tune . . ." ✦ Peter Bogdanovich, *Tom Petty and the Heartbreakers: Runnin' Down a Dream*, ed. Warren Zanes (San Francisco, Calif.: Chronicle, 2007), 107.

69 "The thing about vocals . . ." ✦ David M. Gotz, "Interview: Petty Gets His Torpedoes Together and Damns Ahead to the Airwaves," *Record Review*, February 1980.

SONG LYRICS: VERSE 4

70 "I thought it was a . . ." ✦ Tom Petty and the Heartbreakers, *Playback*, liner notes by Bill Flanagan, MCA Records, 1995.

71 "I'm still thrilled about her" ✦ Andrea M. Rotondo, *Tom Petty: Rock 'n' Roll Guardian* (New York: Overlook Omnibus, 2014), 170.

71 "a real thrill" ✦ Paul Zollo, *Conversations with Tom Petty* (New York: Omnibus, 2005), 214.

71 "great thrill" ✦ Zollo, *Conversations with Tom Petty*, 101.

71 "such a thrill" ✦ Zollo, *Conversations with Tom Petty*, 104.

71 "really a thrill" ✦ Zollo, *Conversations with Tom Petty*, 277.

71–72 "Anytime you get to work . . ." ✦ Zollo, *Conversations with Tom Petty*, 138.

72 "It was the best look . . ." ✦ Tom Matthews, "Heart Breaker," *Milwaukee Magazine*, November 22, 2010.

72 "[Howie] had him for years . . ." ✦ Zollo, *Conversations with Tom Petty*, 173.

72 "maybe a man's king when . . ." ✦ Rotondo, *Tom Petty*, 182.

73 "I think I'm going to . . ." ✦ Rotondo, *Tom Petty*, 141.

SONG LYRICS: CHORUS 2

74 "sometimes if you do that . . ." ✦ Paul Zollo, *Conversations with Tom Petty* (New York: Omnibus, 2005), 216.

75 "The guy in those songs . . ." ✦ Andrea M. Rotondo, *Tom Petty: Rock 'n' Roll Guardian* (New York: Overlook Omnibus, 2014), 98.

75 "it was reaching a point . . ." ✦ Mikal Gilmore, "Positively Dylan," *Rolling Stone*, July 17, 1986.

75 "It took us all getting . . ." ✦ Sandy Robertson, "Petty Prime," *Sounds*, April 20, 1985.

75 "there's some hope in it . . ." ✦ Zollo, *Conversations with Tom Petty*, 221.

MOB SCENE: THEIRS

87 "the biggest crowd I've ever . . ." ✦ Paul Zollo, *Conversations with Tom Petty* (New York: Omnibus, 2005), 9.

87–88 "We watched [Elvis] shoot this . . ." ✦ Zollo, *Conversations with Tom Petty*, 9.

88 "the girls screaming—I never . . ." ✦ Joe Bosso, "American Idols," *Guitar World*, May 2004.

88 "I had a Wurlitzer with . . ." ✦ Andrea M. Rotondo, *Tom Petty: Rock 'n' Roll Guardian* (New York: Overlook Omnibus, 2014), 41.

88 "I used to get in fights . . ." ✦ Blair Jackson, "There's a Lot More to the Heartbreakers Than Tom Petty," *BAM*, January 28, 1983.

88–89 "We butted heads a lot . . ." ✦ Zollo, *Conversations with Tom Petty*, 49.

89 "Look man, you can call . . ." ✦ Jackson, "Blair. (1983, January 28). There's a Lot More."

89 "I've heard this story about . . ." ✦ Jim DeRogatis, *Milk It!* (Cambridge, Mass.: DaCapo, 2003), 49.

89 "Call me a punk again . . ." ✦ Nick Thomas, *Tom Petty: An American Rock and Roll Story* (Green, Ohio: Guardian Express Media, 2014), 63–64.

89 "I really felt distant from . . ." ✦ David M. Gotz, "Interview: Tom Petty," *Record Review*, August 1979.

89–90 "We haven't played bars in . . ." ✦ Gotz, "Interview."

90 "It was in '78 that . . ." ✦ Rotondo, *Tom Petty*, 88.

90 "I really thought I was . . ." ✦ Zollo, *Conversations with Tom Petty*, 68.

90 "It was very violent . . ." ✦ Rotondo, *Tom Petty*, 88.

91 "I've noticed that I can't get . . ." ✦ David Rensin, "20 Questions: Tom Petty," *Playboy*, September 1982.

91 "Ever since then I've been . . ." ✦ Zollo, *Conversations with Tom Petty*, 68.

91 "It's like one minute you're . . ." ✦ Zollo, *Conversations with Tom Petty*, 68.

91 "The second night was maybe . . ." ✦ Joel Selvin, "They've Had Enough: Just for Now," *San Francisco Chronicle*, February 16, 1997.

91 "I remember being shut down . . ." ✦ Mike Snider, "Tom Petty's Live Legacy Gets the Mega-Big-Box Treatment," *USA Today*, December 20, 2009.

91–92 "When we toured [*Long After Dark*] . . ." ✦ Tom Petty and the Heartbreakers, *Playback*, liner notes by Bill Flanagan, MCA Records, 1995.

92 "got in a big fight . . ." ✦ Rotondo, *Tom Petty*, 174.

92 "Well, you know us . . ." ✦ Bill Flanagan, "The Heartbreakers Highway," *Musician*, April 1990.

MOB SCENE: MYSTICISM

93 "Petty's commitment to rock 'n' roll . . ." ✦ Andrea M. Rotondo, *Tom Petty: Rock 'n' Roll Guardian* (New York: Overlook Omnibus, 2014), 81.

93 "When I met Elvis . . ." ✦ Tom Petty, "What I've Learned," *Esquire Magazine*, August 2006.

93 "Elvis appeared like a vision . . ." ✦ Rotondo, *Tom Petty*, 24.

94 "It's all powerful testimony . . ." ✦ Mikal Gilmore, "Tom Petty's Rock Fervor," *Rolling Stone*, June 30, 1977.

94 "You go to these shows . . ." ✦ Paul Zollo, *Conversations with Tom Petty* (New York: Omnibus, 2005), 185.

94 "Maybe the reason it's taken . . ." ✦ Richard Hogan, "Tom Petty Makes 'Hard Promises' to Rock & Roll," *Circus*, August 31, 1981.

94 "he worried that he'd turn . . ." ✦ Rotondo, *Tom Petty*, 103.

94 "I spent a lot of time . . ." ✦ Peter Bogdanovich, *Tom Petty and the Heartbreakers: Runnin' Down a Dream*, ed. Warren Zanes (San Francisco, Calif.: Chronicle, 2007), 153.

95 "It's one of those crazy things . . ." ✦ Bogdanovich, *Tom Petty and the Heartbreakers*, 152.

95 "When my mind drifts toward . . ." ✦ Bogdanovich, *Tom Petty and the Heartbreakers*, 153.

95 "we're all we've got . . ." ✦ Bogdanovich, *Tom Petty and the Heartbreakers*, 152.

95 "[The arson] was so vicious . . ." ✦ Rotondo, *Tom Petty*, 140.

95 "I was pretty turbulent . . ." ✦ Zollo, *Conversations with Tom Petty*, 50.

95–96 "I had taken intensity about . . ." ✦ Rotondo, *Tom Petty*, 123.

96 I gotta say, when we . . ." ✦ Mitch Potter, "Tom Petty: Mellowing of a Rebel," *Toronto Star*, June 11, 1981.

STANDARDS: INDIVIDUALISM

121 "I'm pretty rough on myself . . ." ✦ David Fricke, "It's Good to Be the King," *Rolling Stone*, December 10, 2009.

121 "I know what the objective . . ." ✦ Fricke, "It's good to be the king."

121 "You can accomplish a goal . . ." ✦ David Fricke, introduction, *Tom Petty: The Ultimate Guide to His Music and Legend*, *Rolling Stone* special tribute edition, 2017, 7.

121 "Petty was a student of . . ." ✦ Warren Zanes, *Petty: The Biography* (New York: Henry Holt, 2015), 178.

121–122 "You know, before The Beatles . . ." ✦ Paul Zollo, *Conversations with Tom Petty*, 80.

122 "I sort of like the idea . . ." ✦ Zollo, *Conversations with Tom Petty*, 80.

122 "rock & roll is just . . ." ✦ Mikal Gilmore, "Real-Life Nightmares," *Rolling Stone*, February 1, 1980.

122 "[The rock press] saved my . . ." ✦ Gilmore, "Real-Life Nightmares."

122 "He thinks he's a lousy . . ." ✦ Steve Pond, "Hard Way," *Rolling Stone*, July 23, 1981.

122–123 "I felt terrible. I felt . . ." ✦ Pond, "Hard Way."

123 "It's gotten where everything has . . ." ✦ Neil Strauss, "Last Dance," *Rolling Stone*, June 13, 2006.

123 "my mind is so delicate . . ." ✦ Strauss, "Last Dance."

123 "got more popular, the industry . . ." ✦ Zollo, *Conversations with Tom Petty*, 85–86.

123 "Petty is not like other . . ." ✦ Strauss, "Last Dance."

124 "I see that man going . . ." ✦ Albert Camus, *The Myth of Sisyphus and Other Essays*, trans. Justin O'Brien (New York: Alfred A. Knopf, 1955; rpt., New York: Vintage, 1991), 23. Originally published in France as *Le Mythe de Sisyphe* by Librairie Gallimard, 1942.

124 "Often the best interviews are . . ." ✦ Strauss, "Last Dance."

124 "What can you do if . . ." ✦ Gilmore, "Real-Life Nightmares."

124 "You're always competing with yourself . . ." ✦ Zollo, *Conversations with Tom Petty*, 207.

125 "Tom's the kind of proud guy . . ." ✦ David Wild, "Back on Top, Believe It or Not," *Rolling Stone*, August 8, 1991.

125 "Well, you've got all your . . ." ✦ Zollo, *Conversations with Tom Petty*, 207.

125 "You've got to stick to . . ." ✦ Zollo, *Conversations with Tom Petty*, 207.

125 "For so much of my . . ." ✦ Fricke, "It's Good to Be."

125 "As successful as [the Heartbreakers] . . ." ✦ Strauss, "Last Dance."

125–126 "Tom's not much different from . . ." ✦ Wild, "Back on Top."

126 "says he doesn't like . . ." ✦ Zanes, *Petty*, 180.

126 "Well, I'm stubborn . . ." ✦ Wild, "Back on Top."

126 "I've had nice moments throughout . . ." ✦ Peter Bogdanovich, *Tom Petty and the Heartbreakers: Runnin' Down a Dream*, ed. Warren Zanes (San Francisco, Calif.: Chronicle, 2007), 167.

126 "He's very mysterious . . ." ✦ Zanes, *Petty*, 152.

127 "I didn't even want to . . ." ✦ Robert Hilburn, "A Petty Mood: A Classic Rocker's Passion Is Refreshed," *Los Angeles Times*, May 24, 1987.

127 "No one interferes with the . . ." ✦ Zanes, *Petty*, 200.

STANDARDS: TRANSCENDENCE

128 "There just weren't that many . . ." ✦ Warren Zanes, *Petty: The Biography* (New York: Henry Holt, 2015), 173.

128 "Good things seem to follow . . ." ✦ Andrea M. Rotondo, *Tom Petty: Rock 'n' Roll Guardian* (New York: Overlook Omnibus, 2014), 134.

128–129 "We played for maybe four hours . . ." ✦ Robert Hilburn, "A Songwriter's Greatest Achievement Is to 'Get Someone to Think about Things,'" *Los Angeles Times*, May 24, 1987.

129 "A collaboration with an artist . . ." ✦ Zanes, *Petty*, 196.

129 "No master plan . . ." ✦ Peter Bogdanovich, *Tom Petty and the Heartbreakers: Runnin' Down a Dream*, ed. Warren Zanes (San Francisco, Calif.: Chronicle, 2007), 153.

129 "No one in the Heartbreakers . . ." ✦ Zanes, *Petty*, 203.

129 "It was fun again . . ." ✦ Hilburn, "Songwriter's Greatest Achievement."

129 "'Here's the song . . ." ✦ Jon Bream, "The Many Faces of Bob Dylan," *Minneapolis–St. Paul Star Tribune*, June 22, 1986.

129 "was alternately amazing and frustrating . . ." ✦ Bogdanovich, *Tom Petty and the Heartbreakers*, 149.

129 "Onstage, I felt like he . . ." ✦ Zanes, *Petty*, 202.

129–130 "Among the band members . . ." ✦ Zanes, *Petty*, 201.

130 "He comes in and goes . . ." ✦ Zanes, *Petty*, 204.

130 "From that point forward ..." ◆ Zanes, *Petty*, 213.

130 "he kicked off his most ..." ◆ Robert Hilburn, "Dylan, Petty Open Tour: On Track on Highway '86," *Los Angeles Times*, June 11, 1986.

130 "Dylan—wearing a loose-fitting white ..." ◆ Hilburn, "Dylan, Petty Open Tour."

130–131 "Everyone involved knew that ..." ◆ Zanes, *Petty*, 205.

131 "I just felt really free ..." ◆ Hilburn, "Songwriter's Greatest Achievement."

131 "One reason for Dylan's more ..." ◆ Hilburn, "Dylan, Petty Open Tour."

131 "Tom's finally getting some recognition ..." ◆ David Wild, "Back on Top, Believe It or Not. *Rolling Stone*, August 8, 1991.

132 "suggests nothing short of a ..." ◆ Zanes, *Petty*, 201.

132 "In his book ..." ◆ David Fricke, "It's Good to Be the King," *Rolling Stone*, December 10, 2009.

132 "When I interviewed Bob in December ..." ◆ Robert Hilburn, *Cornflakes with John Lennon* (New York: Rodale, 2010), 235.

132–133 "If he was at the ..." ◆ Paul Zollo, *Conversations with Tom Petty* (New York: Omnibus, 2005), 105.

133 "I feel that we had ..." ◆ Zollo, *Conversations with Tom Petty*, 105.

133 "If I convince myself that ..." ◆ Albert Camus, *The Myth of Sisyphus and Other Essays*, trans. Justin O'Brien (New York: Alfred A. Knopf, 1955; rpt., New York: Vintage, 1991), 21. Originally published in France as *Le Mythe de Sisyphe* by Librairie Gallimard, 1942.

133 "Breaking all the records ..." ◆ Camus, *Myth of Sisyphus*, 21.

134 "The Heartbreakers help Dylan ..." ◆ Hilburn, "Dylan, Petty Open Tour."

134 "After a lot of years ..." ◆ Wild, "Back on Top."

134–135 "I got a lot of ..." ◆ Neil Strauss, "Last Dance," *Rolling Stone*, June 13, 2006.

135 "It is essential to die ..." ◆ Camus, *Myth of Sisyphus*, 19.

135 "I asked him if the ..." ◆ Hilburn, *Cornflakes with John Lennon*, 235.

135 "Imagine the odds against writing ..." ◆ Robert Hilburn, "Dylan and Petty Stage a Triumph at the Forum," *Los Angeles Times*, August 5, 1986.

135 "toughened social attitude and more ..." ◆ Robert Hilburn, "Petty Puts Focus on Social Ills," *Los Angeles Times*, June 8, 1987.

136 "Leaning on influences is common . . ." ◆ Robert Hilburn, "Active or Passive: Two Rock Voices," *Los Angeles Times*, February 4, 1979.

STANDARDS: ABSURDITY

137 "Does the Absurd dictate death?" ◆ Albert Camus, *The Myth of Sisyphus and Other Essays*, trans. Justin O'Brien (New York: Alfred A. Knopf, 1955; rpt., New York: Vintage, 1991), 3. Originally published in France as *Le Mythe de Sisyphe* by Librairie Gallimard, 1942.

137 "'We *know* the songs,' said . . ." ◆ Steve Hochman and Tom Petty, "If It's Monday, This Must Be Miami," *Rolling Stone*, October 5, 1989.

137 "Petty has never made it . . ." ◆ Steve Pond, "The Hard Way," *Rolling Stone*, July 23, 1981.

138 "Bob Dylan, dressed for the . . ." ◆ Geoff Boucher, "Who Is Robert Hilburn? A Champion and an Advocate," *Los Angeles Times*, October 11, 2009.

138 "There were plenty of other . . ." ◆ Boucher, "Who Is Robert Hilburn?"

138 "There are lots of ways . . ." ◆ Robert Hilburn, *Cornflakes with John Lennon* (New York: Rodale, 2010), 209.

138 "There are only two main . . ." ◆ Robert Hilburn, "Active or Passive: Two Rock Voices," *Los Angeles Times*, February 4, 1979.

139 "The Clash is Active . . ." ◆ Hilburn, "Active or Passive."

139 "Passive bands can do enticing . . ." ◆ Hilburn, "Active or Passive."

139 "I guess you just call it . . ." ◆ Robert Hilburn, "A Songwriter's Greatest Achievement Is to 'Get Someone to Think about Things,'" *Los Angeles Times*, May 24, 1987.

139 "there isn't always just one . . ." ◆ Hilburn, "Active or Passive."

139 "the technique of Passive outfits . . ." ◆ Hilburn, "Active or Passive."

139 "I draw from the absurd . . ." ◆ Camus, *Myth of Sisyphus*, 22.

139–140 "His early championing led to . . ." ◆ Boucher, "Who Is Robert Hilburn?"

140 "The joke in the newsroom . . ." ◆ Boucher, "Who Is Robert Hilburn?"

140 "Springsteen's music may rely on . . ." ◆ Robert Hilburn, "Springsteen Finds Ally in Floridian," *Sarasota Journal*, November 13, 1979.

140 "The critic at the *L.A. Times* . . ." ◆ Peter Bogdanovich, *Tom Petty and the Heartbreakers: Runnin' Down a Dream*, ed. Warren Zanes (San Francisco, Calif.: Chronicle, 2007), 61.

140–141 "Petty and the Heartbreakers is . . ." ✦ Robert Hilburn, "Pop Music Review: S. F. Smitten by Heartbreakers," *Los Angeles Times*, April 26, 1977.

141 "A record has to be . . ." ✦ Hilburn, "Pop Music Review: S.F. Smitten."

141 "He and the Heartbreakers band . . ." ✦ Robert Hilburn, "Pop Music Review: Classic Rock of Tom Petty," *Los Angeles Times*, June 7, 1978.

141 "It's complicated now because . . ." ✦ David Fricke, introduction, *Tom Petty: The Ultimate Guide to His Music and Legend*, *Rolling Stone* special tribute edition, 2017, 74.

141 "It's almost wrong of you . . ." ✦ Fricke, *Tom Petty: The Ultimate Guide*, 79.

142 "Yeah, we still do that . . ." ✦ Hochman and Petty, "If It's Monday."

142 "I told all the lawyers . . ." ✦ Cameron Crowe, "Tom Petty's Gonna Get It!" *Rolling Stone*, October 19, 1978.

142 "Sometimes I feel really gracious . . ." ✦ Crowe, "Tom Petty's gonna get it!"

142–143 "The theme of permanent revolution . . ." ✦ Camus, *Myth of Sisyphus*, 18–19.

143 "I don't think I've been . . ." ✦ Mikal Gilmore, "Real-Life Nightmares," *Rolling Stone*, February 21, 1980.

143 "One always finds one's burden . . ." ✦ Camus, *Myth of Sisyphus*, 24.

143 "I don't think I'm a . . ." ✦ David Fricke, "It's Good to Be the King," *Rolling Stone*, December 10, 2009.

144 "Well, see? Things can work . . ." ✦ Stephen Rodrick, "The End of the Line," *Rolling Stone*, July 13–27, 2017.

144 "The cat's just pissed . . ." ✦ Pond, "Hard Way."

144 "Tom Petty is on our side." ✦ Pond, "THard Way.

144 "I was in this defiant . . ." ✦ Robert Hilburn, "Tom Petty Breaks Down 10 of His Songs," *Los Angeles Times*, March 15, 2002.

144 "dark period" ✦ David Wild, "Back on Top, Believe It or Not," *Rolling Stone*, August 8, 1991.

144 "was viewed as a disappointment . . ." ✦ Robert Hilburn, "Tom Petty Tries His Hand at Southern Rock," *Los Angeles Times*, March 31, 1985.

144 "Petty's best early songs . . ." ✦ Hilburn, "Songwriter's Greatest Achievement."

145 "a textbook example of how . . ." ✦ Robert Hilburn, "Album Review: Petty Gets His Message Across," *Sarasota Herald-Tribune*, November 6, 1982.

145 "Petty's ability to weave meaningful . . ." ✦ Hilburn, "Album Review."

145 "The secret is putting your . . ." ✦ Hilburn, "Album Review."

145 "the album's central song" ✦ Hilburn, "Album Review."

145 "not only illustrates the twin . . ." ✦ Hilburn, "Album Review."

145 "is on the surface a . . ." ✦ Hilburn, "Album Review."

145 "Early in the song . . ." ✦ Hilburn, "Album Review."

146 "deeper" and "more convincing" ✦ Hilburn, "Album Review."

146 "The advances in *Long After Dark* . . ." ✦ Hilburn, "Album Review."

146 "Petty's ability to move from . . ." ✦ Hilburn, "Album Review."

146 "For all its crowd-pleasing vigor . . ." ✦ Robert Hilburn, "Petty and Lone Justice Home Again at Forum," *Los Angeles Times*, August 3, 1985.

147 "I feel a little restricted . . ." ✦ Hilburn, "Songwriter's Greatest Achievement."

147 "As a songwriter, the best . . ." ✦ Hilburn, "Songwriter's Greatest Achievement."

147 "Just as one does or . . ." ✦ Camus, *Myth of Sisyphus*, 3.

147 "spoke about the tensions . . ." ✦ Hilburn, "Tom Petty Breaks Down."

147–148 "I like that song a lot . . ." ✦ Hilburn, "Tom Petty Breaks Down."

148 "Rock fans adopt heroes . . ." ✦ Robert Hilburn, "10 Years Later: A Critic's List of the Best Albums of the Decade," *Los Angeles Times*, May 17, 1987.

148 "as old as rock & roll . . ." ✦ Fricke, "It's Good to Be."

148 "It's tough when you look . . ." ✦ Wild, "Back on Top."

148–149 "Getting recognized does a real . . ." ✦ Hilburn, "Pop Music Review: S. F. Smitten."

149 "I hate being expected to . . ." ✦ Hilburn, "Tom Petty Tries His Hand."

149 "That revolt gives life its . . ." ✦ Camus, *Myth of Sisyphus*, 19.

149 "Rather than tailor his style . . ." ✦ Hilburn, "Tom Petty Breaks Down."

Music of the American South

Lightning Source UK Ltd.
Milton Keynes UK
UKHW020656280822
407873UK00002B/348